BEFORE THE STORM

WAR OF THE SUBMARINE: BOOK 0

R.G. ROBERTS

To Erin, without whom this entire universe would not exist.

To my wonderful wife, Shira, whose support has been priceless while I begin this publishing journey.

*And finally, to all my brothers and sisters from the Wick, who live and die by the motto: **"I will try."***

Contents

Prologue: Deep Sea Devils

5 August 2037, 100 nautical miles south of Osborn Station, in the Indian Ocean

Danielle Thayer had the best job in the world.

Her father, overprotective pastor that he was, thought she was an undersea miner at the nearby Olhuveli Resort and Mining Consortium, where she *had* been employed for six months as a team lead. In fact, she was the one who found Olhuveli's famous Star Mine, the largest underwater diamond mine in the world. And what did she get for that?

Nada.

Unless you counted getting propositioned by her supervisor. She got a good groping and a "friendly" invitation she couldn't turn down. That her into his quarters and the opportunity to steal his access codes. That got her a cold hundred grand out of the consortium's miscellaneous expense account, not to mention the a Proteus submersible luxury yacht she stole as a side-bonus. Then she set out to make her fortune.

Six months later, after selling that cute little submarine for ten million American dollars—it was worth more than that, but you took what you could get on the black market—and worked a few other odd jobs, Danielle hooked up with some like-minded fellows on a new career path.

"Step into the life raft and no one gets hurt," she said, cradling her AK-47. A semi-automatic rifle was a bad weapon for underwater environments, but Danielle liked to shoot, and it sure did intimidate people.

"Look, I can pay you whatever you want," the businessman said for the fourteenth time.

He was tall, fat, balding, and British. Danielle hadn't bothered to learn his name, because so far, he was just like the others. She sighed.

"Yeah, because we're out here because we like traceable money." She smiled sweetly. "Tell me another one, sugar. Step into the life raft, unless you want to take a real long swim."

"I can pay you in Bitcoin—"

"The feds got in that business last decade, bucko. Get a move on."

Barsati, her helmsman, snickered from behind her. "Listen to the boss lady. She's the nice one."

Glancing down, Danielle judged the gap between her boat and the Phoenix 2000 owned by the Brits. The Phoenix was a hundred-million-dollar boat, the biggest payday her group ever scored. Its smooth lines were white, every bit polished or newly painted, right down to the perfect glass windows.

Yeah, this was it. This was the big one, the one that would let her buy a real submarine, one that would scare the fools on every independent station in the area. There was a *Kilo*-class submarine on the market, a Russian relic bought by India and later sold to Myanmar. Now it was up for grabs, and Danielle would make it hers.

You didn't need to be a country to have a warship these days. You just needed vision and determination to reach your goals.

Danielle pushed the businessman into the life raft. He landed with a squeak and a scream; maybe he broke his leg. She didn't care. Assuming he spent as much money on the raft as he did the submarine, there should be a medical kit in there. If not, well, that was his poor judgement.

His husband and friends followed before she could push anybody else.

Apparently, no one fancied a swim.

Their loss.

Chapter 1

New Threats

22 August 2037, in the Laccadive Sea

The submarine's hull cracked open like an egg when it hit the bottom, leaving ample room for a school of rainbow runner fish to swim through what used to be the control room. The chasm was big enough for divers, too—if a little dangerous, and macabre, if you drove submarines for a living.

Alex Coleman was all right with that. As an experienced diver, he spent as much time as he could underwater *outside* a submarine, though he made an exception for this one. The old *Kilo*-class submarine lay on her side, the victim of an exploded battery that took out an airlock and personnel tube three years earlier at nearby Alderman's.

Mercifully, the investigators removed the bodies long ago. The crew back aft in the engineering compartment even survived, thanks to a quick combined rescue force from Alderman's Underwater Depot and the Maldives. Critical equipment was gone, too, either at the request of the Myanmar government or taken by scavengers stupid enough to think they could make it work again.

Swimming forward, Alex eyed the watertight hatch at the back of the control room as three members of his dive group swam through it. No way was he dumb enough to go back there. Swimming in enclosed spaces was a good way to get trapped; just last year, two inexperienced British tourists drowned in the crew quarters. Diving for fifteen years taught Alex not to go places he might not come back from, so he stayed in the control room instead.

After all, *Kilo*-class submarines might be old, but nine world navies still used them—and most of them weren't very friendly with the United States. Seeing the inside of a *Kilo* was fascinating from a professional front—and it was a cool place to dive during his time off.

After a few more minutes of poking around, Alex headed back to the north Alderman's dive lock. Dying in some other country's submarine would be a really stupid way to go, and Alex's air was running low.

He swam through the dive lock and into the transition pool, but when Alex breached the surface, Lieutenant Sue Grippo extended a towel to him with a scowl.

"We've got trouble, XO," she said.

"And here I was thinking about going for a drink." Alex pulled himself out of the water and removed his fins. "Who was it this time?"

Play time was over. Time to return to being Lieutenant Commander Coleman, the Executive Officer of USS *Kansas* (SSN 810). Sighing, Alex ran his mind through a mental list of problem sailors, taking silent bets on who pissed off the locals or otherwise managed to do a dirty. But Sue shook her head.

"Not a who so much as a what. We got a flash tasker, and the captain sent me to get you pronto." Sue shrugged. "Sounds like some pirates are messing with underwater stations, so they want a sub to investigate."

"Not here, I trust?"

Alex let his eyes sweep over the interior of the transition area. The pool was enormous and saltwater; the dive lock at the bottom led right out to the Laccadive Sea, which lay between India and the Maldives. However, one floor above this housed a busy and constantly growing resort, tucked in between dual gold mines and four oil-rich wells.

Alderman's was one of the Indian Ocean's larger underwater stations, owned by an alliance of corporations based in the Maldives, India, and China. Security here was tight, tighter than on most navy bases Alex had been based on. Imagining some two-bit pirates stealing more than a pizza here was hard. You couldn't walk six feet without running into security—even down here in the dive area, there were six visible cameras.

And probably more cameras we can't *see*, he thought behind a smile.

"No, sir. We've got more information on board," Sue replied.

"I can take a hint." Fins off, Alex levered himself to his feet. "I assume I've got time to change my clothes, or do I have to run to the boat barefoot?"

Sue laughed. "The captain didn't say it was that urgent, sir, but he did say we're getting underway in the morning."

"Good, I always like it when I get to keep my dignity." Chuckling, Alex waved Sue away as he headed towards the locker room. "I'll meet you on the boat."

Twenty minutes later, Alex turned in his rented scuba gear—storing pressurized tanks on a submarine was against Navy regs—and headed to the airlock connecting *Kansas* to Alderman's.

He ignored the way a quartet of locals glared at him on his way by. One muttered something about American overreach, but they looked away when Alex eyed then back. He shook his head and headed for the boat. American popularity, or lack thereof, was not his problem.

Mating an attack submarine to an underwater station was a new art. In fact, coming to Alderman's was only Alex's second time *ever* doing so—the first was back at Jack Black's off the east coast of South Carolina when *Kansas'* emergency diesel blew a bearing during training.

Alderman's was shallow enough that *Kansas* sat on the bottom when connected to the station. Two rigid tubes held the pair together, joined at *Kansas'* forward and aft hatch. Both entrances were guarded by tired sailors who would've preferred to still be in one of Alderman's three bars instead of being on duty. Alex headed to the forward tunnel, nodding when the senior sailor there saluted him.

"Captain and COB are back on board already, sir," Chief Darcey Martelle said.

"Thanks, Chief."

Alex slipped into the tunnel, sealing the airlock behind himself and listening to the hiss while it pressurized. Fifteen seconds later, he stepped into the tube and put his game face on. Liberty was over; he was back to being the Executive Officer, or second-in-command, on board USS *Kansas*, one of the U.S. Navy's newest *Virginia*-class attack submarines.

Kansas wasn't the newest boat in the rapidly expanding American navy, but she was a good sub with a great crew. They trained hard, played hard, and now, a month into deployment to the Indian Ocean, they finally had a real job to do.

Not that lurking around tracking Chinese nuclear submarines wasn't a real job. It was just that the Chinese boats were *loud*, and it wasn't much of a challenge. *Kansas* was ready for more.

Dumping his stuff in his stateroom, Alex threw on a set of coveralls and went to the wardroom. *Kansas'* officers' mess was also their meeting place; aside from the mess decks, it was the one place large enough to hold a meeting. In battle—not that the U.S. engaged in a good, old-fashioned submarine war since World War II—it also doubled as a tiny hospital.

Commander William Rothberg waited for him. Rothberg looked more like a librarian than he did a warfighter, complete with the early balding and thick, government-issue glasses. He also had a love of submarine food and a hatred of exercise that kept him a tad portly, but Rothberg was smart, competent, and—if rumor was right—going places.

Alex was his captain's physical opposite: light-skinned, blond-haired, and skinny enough that nobody would mistake him for some gunslinging warfighter, either. They were of a height, which meant they were taller than Lieutenant Sue Grippo, who joined them before Alex could even greet his commanding officer.

"Glad you didn't get stuck in that submarine, Alex." Rothberg grinned. "We've got another *Kilo* to hunt, but this one's not on the bottom. Yet."

Rothberg gestured both officers into chairs; Alex plopped down to his right. "Pirates in a *Kilo?* They steal it or buy it?"

"Sounds like someone got Russian military surplus back in the day and then sold it." Rothberg shrugged. "Who they bought it from isn't our concern—finding them and stopping them is."

"Not that I mind the idea of hunting pirates, Captain, but isn't that usually a surface skimmer job?" Alex cocked his head. "It's not like we're going to go *boarding* them, or that we've got the space for prisoners if we do catch them."

The very idea of trying to somehow connect *Kansas* with a smaller diesel submarine like a *Kilo*-class boat while underwater was enough to make Alex's head spin. It'd be like mating a cat with a porcupine, just less efficient.

"The U.N. thinks we'll be stealthier, and Seventh Fleet agrees," Rothberg said, referring to the fleet that owned U.S. Navy assets in the Indian Ocean. "Ours is not to reason why—we just need to find these bastards and end them."

Sue frowned. "Captain?"

"We've got a video of these...gentlemen tearing through part Victorie Station." Rothberg scowled. "Victorie Station—in case you need to look it up, because I did—is actually seven different underwater hubs, each of which drills the shit out of oil. It's the world's biggest oil exporter, and, you guessed it, the pirates stole a bunch of it. After killing seventeen people."

"Killing?" Sue blinked. "I thought modern-day pirates held people for ransom?"

"Apparently, these yokels are cut from a different cloth. Here, watch." Rothberg brought a video up on the big screen covering the forward bulkhead. It was flanked by mementos of *Kansas'* various port visits—not too many, since the boat was only seven years old and this just her second deployment—and a signed football from the Superbowl winning Kansas City Chiefs.

The video flickered and then rolled into action, showing a crowd of people in a cramped space, muttering nervously. The blue cast to the lights told Alex they were underwater; he didn't know why every underwater station designer thought blue lights were chic, but the damn things were in vogue. The Rush to the Ocean Floor might have opened up underwater real estate in a big way, but it hadn't made the landscape *pretty*, that was for sure.

"Stay back, and nobody gets hurt!" an accented voice shouted. "Stay back!"

Two figures to the right manipulated a fuel cross-connect; Alex remembered from his pre-deployment briefs that Victorie Station Quatre was one of the two refineries in the seven-part underwater conglomerate.

"Are you done yet?" A third figure asked. She was closer to the camera, tall and dark-haired. She wore a tank on her back, one Alex initially took for an air tank, but then he spotted the gun-like object in her hands.

"Oh, shit," he whispered.

"Ten minutes," one of the guys transferring fuel replied.

Glaring, the pirate leader turned back to the crowd. People pushed others; the muttering grew louder. Finally, one man pushed to the front.

"Look, we don't want trouble, but—"

"Stay back!" The pirate woman gestured with the flamethrower.

The crowd pressed forward.

"Stay back!"

Someone shouted in French. Another in a language Alex didn't recognize. The pirate woman didn't offer a fourth warning—

She opened up with the flame thrower.

Flames engulfed the crowd. Screams filled the air; the front line of terrified people tried to push back, but those behind them were slower to react. The front ranks couldn't get away. People went down, screaming, pleading, cursing.

Bile rose in Alex's throat as those at the back of the crowd fled. He could imagine the smell of charred flesh in the recycled air or an underwater station, like people burning in a can. His stomach rolled.

Rothberg cut the video. "As you can see, these aren't your run of the mill thieves. We think—"

A sharp knock interrupted the captain off. Lieutenant (junior grade) Chris King, *Kansas'* assistant navigator, opened the wardroom door and stuck his head in. "Sorry to interrupt, Captain, but there's a bunch of Marines here saying they have orders to come aboard."

"Marines?" Alex echoed.

Rothberg smiled. "If we find these people, we're going to need muscle. Seventh Fleet didn't say *who* they would send, but they did indicate someone was coming."

"I'd rather SEALs," Sue said. "At least they know their way around a submarine."

Every boat in the fleet worked with SEALs from time to time. The Navy's special warfare teams frequently swam on or off submarines for their missions. The relationship between SEALs and submariners was sometimes contentious and often awkward, but at better the devil you knew.

Alex had a bad feeling about this. "I'll get them situated, sir," he said. As XO, the little details were his job. Everything was his problem, from where guests slept to the plan of the day.

His eyes slid to the paused video before Alex could stop them. He made himself look away, trying not to think about seventeen people *burned* to death. Shaking himself, Alex ducked out of the wardroom and made for the forward ladder. Going up that ladder to move sideways into the personnel tube always struck him as weird, but it was drier than swimming.

Raised voices reached him before the airlock finished cycling to let Alex back into the station.

"With all due respect, sir, without orders, I can't let you on board or provide you with berthing." Lieutenant Penelope Juno was *Kansas'* supply officer, a tiny red-haired firecracker under the best of circumstances.

These were not the best circumstances.

"Hey, if my printed orders aren't enough for you, Lieutenant, I'd be happy to call General Avilla," a deep male voice replied.

"Sir, printed orders can be faked." *Tap, tap, tap*; that was the sound of Penny's impatient foot against the steel floor of Anderman's. "We can only accept properly transmitted orders."

"Lieutenant, my team and I didn't just spend twenty hours in a plane to turn around and go home."

The airlock door slid open with a hiss. Alex strode out as the marine lieutenant colonel facing Penny crossed his massive arms. The marine dwarfed Penny by at least a foot, and he was twice as wide as her, too. Twenty camouflage-wearing Marines stood behind him, carrying seabags and rucksacks full of gear, along with weapons they probably didn't want Alderman's to know about.

Kansas' pair of watchstanders were behind Penny, tensely aware that they were outnumbered and outgunned. Alex slipped between them, blinking when he caught sight of the senior marine's face.

"I should have known you'd be the one creating trouble, Paul." Alex crossed his arms.

"Alex fucking Coleman," the giant rumbled. "If there was ever a submarine I *wouldn't* want to spend time on, it'd be yours."

Alex cocked his head. "Will you even fit?"

"With all this gear? Fuck if I know. You squids get to find somewhere to put it."

Penny watched the pair warily, her eyes snapping back and forth. "XO, I still don't have orders for these guys."

"It's all right, Suppo. I know this unfortunate example of a marine officer." Alex grinned, turning back to Paul. "And I also know that he wouldn't be here for shits and giggles. He's going to hit his head on everything and use up Doc's stock of Band-Aids. He might be built like a gorilla, but he cries like a three-year-old when he's hurt."

"Damn right I am." Paul stepped forward to trap Alex in a bone-crushing hug. "Shit, it's good to see you, Rook Buddy."

"You too, asshole." Alex laughed, slapping his college roommate on the back. "Come on, let's get you and your people stowed. Then I'll start the betting pool on how many times you hit your head."

"Is it too late to ask for another submarine?"

Chapter 2

Old Friends

"If you weren't joking about that betting pool, you owe me a cut," Lieutenant Colonel Paul Swanson said a few hours later. "And why the hell am I in the *top* rack? I feel like a sardine."

"You'd feel like a sardine wherever I put you," Alex replied from where he sat at the computer in his cramped stateroom.

Space was at a premium in every submarine, even a large attack sub like *Kansas.* Cramming twenty-nine marines in—two of which were officers—meant that Alex got a roommate, which he didn't usually have. Tradition said the XO hosted the senior "rider" on a submarine; his luck said it was his college roommate and old friend.

Random draw put rugby player and wannabe special forces marine Paul Swanson and skinny nerd/engineer Alex Coleman together during their freshmen year at Norwich University. David and Goliath comparisons were quick to follow, but they didn't really line up. Paul was smart—contrary to what people thought, the Marine Corps didn't let meatheads command battalions of Recon

Marines—and Alex wasn't a physical nincompoop. He just didn't lift barbells for fun.

Nobody expected the pair to hit it off, or for them to continue rooming together for the next four years. Paul was with him when Alex almost got expelled for creating—and exploding—coffee creamer fireballs their senior year. And Alex dragged Paul back from a memorable encounter with midshipmen from the Coast Guard Academy before faces got broken and futures ruined.

Conflicting career commitments kept them on opposite sides of the country for much of the last fifteen years, until a handful of annoying pirates threw them back together.

"The bottom rack looks bigger." Paul flipped to his stomach, scowling.

"It's not." Alex rolled his eyes. "And I sleep in that rack every day, so you can't have it. You're just here for a couple of weeks."

"Wah wah wah. All this being crammed into a metal tube with seamen all the time must really ruin your sense of humor."

"Wow, I've *never* heard that one before."

"Okay, so I'm not at my best. It's weird down here, and this place wasn't built for people like me."

"Yeah, you're about a foot taller and two times wider than the average submariner." Alex chuckled. "But you've been on a sub before, Paul. Remember our midshipmen cruise?"

"I hated it then, too. *Please* tell me there's somewhere I can work out."

"Same torpedo room your guys are sleeping in, yeah." The two women were in the tiny female berthing back aft, but the men were in *Kansas'* overflow berthing—which was the torpedo room.

"You don't even have a *gym?*" Paul buried his face in the pillow. "This is fucking uncivilized."

"You're one to talk, Junior Gorilla."

"Hey, I'm a full-blown gorilla these days and proud of it. My arms are the size of your head."

"You can say that again. Congrats on making O-5, by the way," Alex said. Lieutenant Colonel in the Marine Corps was the equivalent of a full Commander in the Navy, one rank above Alex's.

"Thanks. You can't be far behind, are you?"

"Selected. Got a couple of months before I put it on. Nancy's already got it, of course."

"What a shocker." Paul laughed. "She's always been ahead of us, and never let either of us live it down."

Nancy, Alex's wife, was also their classmate from Norwich University. Unlike Alex and Paul, who managed good enough grades to keep their scholarships and get commissioned as officers, Nancy was an overachiever from the get-go. She still was, too, hitting every career wicket ahead of Alex and always ending up on top of the promotion lists.

Alex was so damned proud of her.

"How're the girls?" Paul asked, referring to Alex's daughters.

"Teenagers." Alex sighed. "Pretty good ones, but don't tell them I said that."

"My lips are sealed. Unless they bribe me, of course. Uncle Paul is *always* susceptible to bribes."

Alex snorted. "Speaking of SEALs, how'd we end up with you guys? Farting about in submarines really isn't Recon's usual thing."

"The boys were busy, so they called up some real men. And women." Paul grinned. "But don't you worry your little nerd ass. Pirates are pirates, no matter how far underwater they hide. We know how to deal with their asses: give them one warning, and if they don't listen, we bring them back in body bags."

Alex wasn't fan of violence, but thinking about those seventeen burnt bodies, he had to agree.

"How's the roommate?" Commander Rothberg asked during his and Alex's nightly sit down.

"Same as always." Alex chuckled. "Paul acts like a meathead, but he's got a pretty good brain."

"You know each other?" Rothberg's eyes crinkled in amusement. "Penny's already talking about your David and Goliath routine."

"Oh, please don't pin that moniker on us, sir. It got old at Norwich."

"You two go that far back?"

"Yeah, we were roommates there, too. Some random algorithm in Jackman Hall probably thought it'd be funny." Alex shrugged. "Joke's on them. Paul's one of the best friends I've ever had. He's damn competent, too—you don't need to worry about him getting the job done. He won't let us down."

"That's good to know. He's already got Penny spooked."

"He's a giant teddy bear whining about how small the top rack is," Alex said. "Tell her to threaten to take his food away, and she'll win every time."

Rothberg laughed. "I'll leave that one for my indefatigable XO. Good command training for you."

"Is that what they call it these days?"

"There are still some mysteries of command you have yet to uncover, my young protégé." Rothberg waved an airy hand. "Charming ship riders into good behavior while reassuring your supply officer is a delicate balance, but I feel you're up to the task."

"It's so nice to have your confidence, sir." Alex laughed. "But speaking of tasks, Nav came to me earlier about MM2 Santos. It sounds like she's serious about cross-rating, and if so..."

"You want to take her out, XO?" Commander Rothberg asked the next morning in *Kansas'* control room.

The small space was even more cramped than usual with the addition of Paul Swanson, who took up more space than any two people combined. But Alex didn't have the heart to tell his old friend to leave, not with the way Paul watched, fascinated, as *Kansas'* sailors ran through the pre-underway checklist.

Besides, watching him cram himself like a sardine into the corner by the fire control consoles was funny.

Control, sometimes called "the Conn," was the nerve center from which the submarine ran. Control stations lined the port, starboard, and forward bulkheads, each with dual monitors, one on top of the other. A touchscreen navigation table was in the middle, not far from the "pilot" seats up forward. Traditionalists still liked to call those chairs the helm and planesmen; the *Virginia*-class had revolutionized American submarine warfare in some ways, but some things never changed.

The sub's navigation detail was manned, except for the topside—*out*side—watches that they typically stationed when leaving port. Instead, they withdrew their personnel tube watchstanders inside the submarine and secured both forward and aft hatches. The submarine still sat in a cradle on the bottom, and the tubes remained attached—otherwise, a shift in current could tip her right over.

Theoretically, subs were weighted towards the bottoms of their keels to prevent that. It still hadn't stopped USS *Kentucky*, *Kansas*' slightly-younger sister ship, from going belly up when departing Yankee Station back in 2033. It took salvage crews three days to free *Kentucky's* sail from Yankee Station's outer wall, and nine people died in the flooding when the station was breached.

Yeah, not a good day for the Navy.

Rothberg, however, trusted Alex not to do the same sort of boneheaded thing that got *Kentucky* stuck to Yankee Station.

"I'd love to, sir," Alex said.

Rothberg grinned and leaned back against the nav table. "Then she's all yours."

"XO, aye." Alex shoved his hands in his pockets and sucked in a deep breath. "Officer of the Deck, are all stations manned and ready?"

"Yes, sir," Sue replied. "Maneuvering reports ready to answer all bells."

"Very well." Alex lifted his handheld radio. "Alderman Operations, this is Warship Eight-One-Zero. Please retract your tubes, over."

"This is Alderman Operations, roger, standby for retraction, over."

"Eight-One-Zero, roger."

Alex tried not to hold his breath. This was the second most dangerous part of the evolution; with the tubes retracted, only the cradle held *Kansas* upright. He turned to Sue. "Standby the outboard."

"Standby the outboard, OOD, aye," she replied.

Repeating commands back was a cornerstone of submarine life. It prevented misunderstandings, even in the heat of battle, and made sure the orders carried out were the ones intended. The nuclear navy was especially particular about it. No U.S. Navy sub ever had a reactor accident, and they aimed to keep it that way.

Alex's radio crackled. "Eight-One-Zero, Alderman Operations, the tubes are retracted, over."

"This is Eight-One-Zero, roger, break, flatten the cradle, over."

"Alderman's Ops, roger, over."

This was the danger point. If *Kansas* didn't get out of the cradle fast enough, or if Alderman's operations team was a touch slow telling them when it was flush with the ocean floor and could no longer support the submarine, *Kansas* could fall right over.

At least two careers would go down the drain if that happened: Alex's for driving the boat into a civilian station, and Rothberg's for letting him.

Kansas rocked slightly.

"Eight-One-Zero, this is Ops. Cradle is flattened, over."

"Ballast us up, Master Chief," Alex ordered. "Make your depth two hundred feet."

"Make my depth two hundred feet, COB, aye," Master Chief Chindeu Casey, the Chief of the Boat replied. He was a *Kansas* old timer, on board longer than Alex, and he knew his stuff. If there was one watchstander Alex didn't need to supervise, it was Casey. Alex left him to do his job.

The depth gauge read 348 feet. Alex watched it and forced himself to wait.

Kansas rocked again, buffeted by underwater currents. Then she rocked again, and finally—

347.

345.

340.

How high were the sides of the cradle? Standard when flattened was zero, but who knew how good the maintenance at Alderman's was. Clipping a side on the way out was a surefire way to tip the boat over and go splat.

335.

"Train your outboard zero-five-zero at one-half speed," Alex ordered. "Ahead one third. Right full ridder."

"Outboard is zero-five-zero at one half," the Chief of the Watch replied immediately.

"Ahead one third, right full rudder, aye," the young sailor at the helm said. "Engines are ahead one third for five knots. My rudder is right thirty degrees, no new course given."

Alex let out the breath and heard it rattle in his chest as he felt *Kansas* lift off. "Very well."

The attack sub crept forward and laterally, with most of her motion to port. The right rudder moved her stern to the left, while the "outboard"—really a bow thruster, but no submariner called it that—moved her bow in the same direction. Ballasting lifted her out of the cradle, and the lateral motion took her away from Alderman's at the same time.

Patience was the name of the game. The currents were pretty benign here; *Kansas'* GPS-determined speed over ground was three knots sideways. Not bad.

"Range to station?" Alex asked.

"Fifteen yards and opening," Sue replied.

"Very well."

Alex let the boat creep sideways for another minute—another hundred yards—before ordering: "Secure and retract the outboard. Rudder amidships."

"Nice driving, XO," Rothberg said as *Kansas'* watchstanders obeyed the orders. "I would've gotten impatient and kicked it up earlier, like I did back at Jack Black's when I almost hit the transfer tube."

Alex chuckled. "I think we can blame them for leaving it out, sir."

"Bullshit. Take the compliment, XO. I know you suck at that, but sometimes, it's nice to be good at your job."

"Um, thank you, sir." Working for Rothberg was a pleasure—the captain gave him every chance to learn and prove himself. Before long, Alex hoped to have his own submarine, and he knew he owned Rothberg for helping him get there.

Rothberg cleared his throat. "All right, folks, while we work our way back into open ocean, let's talk about the mission. By now, everyone's seen the video of the animals we're after. They're driving an old *Kilo*-class submarine of the Russian vintage, so if we're lucky, it'll sink before they can hurt anyone else.

"However, if we aren't that fortunate, our job is to find them, catch them in the act, and then capture said submarine. Preferably with the pirates alive to stand trial, though the U.N. hasn't yet determined which country gets to try them. Clear as mud?"

Everyone murmured assent. Alex spent more time watching their people than he did his captain; he already knew how Rothberg felt. But he saw the same anger and disgust mirrored on every face, Paul's included. If there was one thing every mariner could agree on, it was a mutual hatred of pirates.

Pirates were the scum of the ocean and always had been. These just killed seventeen people, and for what? Fuel? Money? There were a thousand and one ways to get rich under the sea right now, and they chose the ones that included murder.

Yeah, Alex was a-okay with chasing these guys, and so was the rest of *Kansas'* crew. Hell, he'd even hold Paul's hat while his roommate shot the bastards.

Chapter 3

Popularity Contests

24 August 2037, the Indian Ocean

P aul tagged along for Alex's daily messing and berthing inspection (none-too-affectionately called 'heads and beads') the day after *Kansas* got underway. Alex could tell his roommate was antsy. The treadmill in the torpedo room was down for repairs, and even Paul could only lift so many free weights. He attended every meal on the boat—all four of them—and watched movies non-stop, but Paul wasn't built for sitting still.

"You guys get that clogged head fixed?" Alex asked Machinist's Mate First Class Zef Harding, the senior petty officer in Berthing Number One.

The berthing was a narrow space, spanning *Kansas'* entire top deck. Racks, stacked three high, were aligned from port to starboard in narrow rows. Sailors called them "coffin racks." They were barely big enough to flip over in because of the drawer hidden under the mattress. But a rack and a standup locker were the only places a sailor had to store belongs in this home away from home.

Commander Rothberg was a tolerant captain, who didn't mind when his sailors brought comforters and even rack curtains from home. One top rack had a Dallas Cowboys blanket, while the one below it had *Star Wars* curtains and a turtle-shaped pillow. Across from that was a rack decorated with video game posters and another with comic book characters.

"Yes, sir." Harding grinned. "Suzy pulled a K-Bar out of the bottom pipe."

"Say what?" Paul's eyes bulged. He stood crookedly to fit between two racks by the lounge area, which featured three couches and a television.

"People flush stupid shit and it clogs the CHT system," Alex said, turning to look at another sailor. "You keep the knife, Suzy?"

"You bet I did, XO," MM2 Jim Suszynski replied. "Disinfected it first. Good knife. Mine now."

Paul's jaw hung open for several long seconds. "You squids are *weird*."

"This ain't nothing, Colonel," Suzy said. "You should've seen what I found in—"

Alex's radio crackled. "XO, OOD, we have tonals on a submerged *Kilo* at thirty thousand yards."

His heart leapt. "On my way." Alex pointed a finger at the snickering machinist's mates. "You guys get a freebie this time. Don't waste it."

Suzy laughed. "No chance of that, sir."

"C'mon." Alex gestured for Paul to follow him, pretending he didn't hear his friend's sigh of relief when they squeezed out of the berthing compartment.

"Fuck, how do people *live* in there? I might actually suffocate."

Snickering, Alex swung onto the nearest down ladder, moving forward towards control. "Most submariners have the sense not to get as jacked as you are."

"With nothing to do but workout, I can't imagine why more of them don't." Paul rolled his eyes and took the ladder steps two at a time when it was his turn.

"Nothing to do, says the ship rider."

"Hey, give me someone to shoot, and I'll *do* plenty."

Their bickering carried the pair to control, where Alex pulled the watertight door open and stepped through. Fortunately, Paul knew to dog the door down behind himself; Alex could ignore him and take in the tense atmosphere in the attack center.

"*Kilo* bears zero-seven-niner, range thirty-one thousand yards," Senior Chief Salli said from sonar. She wasn't on watch; instead, she leaned over the operators' shoulders, watching the displays and wearing a spare headset.

"Officer of the Deck, come left to zero-seven-niner at ten knots," Rothberg ordered. "Let's creep up on this fellow until we have a positive I.D."

"Officer of the Deck, aye," Lieutenant Sue Grippo turned to give orders to the helmsman as Alex went to the sonar corner, Paul on his heels.

"How we looking, Senior?" he asked.

"It's definitely a *Kilo*, sir, but at over fifteen nautical miles, I can't tell you whose it is until we get a lot closer," Salli replied.

"And there's a fuckton of *Kilos* out here, sir," Master Chief Casey, *Kansas*' Chief of the Boat, said from Salli's left. "Everyone and their drunk maiden aunt has one, because Mother Russia is happy to sell them to you."

"Is that how the pirates got one?" Paul asked.

"Nah, probably the black market, sir," Casey said. "Even Russia ain't that dumb. Or if they are, we'll never prove it."

Casey sided up next to Salli to study the computer screen, frowning. The Master Chief was a sonar operator, too, or had been before he crossed over to become a Chief of the Boat. The Chief of the Boat, or the COB, was the senior enlisted man or woman on a submarine. They were the epitome of a submariner, the highest an enlisted sailor could rise. And while Casey might be a tad rusty at sonar, there was nothing wrong with his brain.

"You can't just lose a submarine." Paul frowned. "Can you?"

"Sure you can, if you're the Russian Federation in the late twentieth or early twenty-first century." Casey snorted. "List it for disposal, pay someone off, bam, fairy dust happens. The *Kilo* vanishes into thin air. We don't know much about the boat these fuckers have, but if it came from Russia, it's probably a Project 877.

"That means the boat was commissioned between 1980 and 1995-ish, 'cause the later boats are all accounted for. Those suckers do last forever, but they get louder as they get older, and we've got good sound profiles on pretty much all of 'em. As a bonus, 'cause the Navy never throws anything out, the computer's still got profiles of supposedly decommissioned boats, too. Just in case."

"You memorized all that for fun?" Paul asked.

"Shit, Colonel, I memorized all that back in sonar school. I cut my teeth tracking these suckers when

I was a kid." Casey laughed. "They used to be considered fairly quiet, back before we got the new filters and computer programs. Back then, we could only bag 'em when they snorted. Now we've got a better chance of getting them while they're submerged, even when running on battery."

"What speed is this guy going?" Alex asked.

"Around seventeen knots, sir," Salli replied. "Not the speed I'd go if I wanted to be stealthy, even in a diesel."

"Diesel?" Paul repeated in an undertone.

"Subs come in three flavors of propulsion," Alex said. "Nuclear powered, like your lovely ride here. Or diesel-electric, like the older *Kilos*—they run on their batteries while submerged and recharge on the surface while snorkeling. Finally we've got, there's air-independent-propulsion. AIP uses fuel cells or an electric motor while submerged instead of batteries, which is equally quiet but lasts a lot longer. The *Kilos* are all too old to be AIP, though. This cat's a diesel, which means he's on batteries. Running around at seventeen knots is a good way to wear the battery down, not to mention get himself noticed like you dropping trou on the U.P. freshman year."

"I could do without remembering that dare, thanks." Paul scratched his chin. "Why not just drive on the surface?"

"Modern subs aren't built for that. Giant metal tubes aren't really great in rough seas—you need a pointy hull for that," Alex said. "World War II boats were designed to run fast on the surface and duck under to hunt the enemy, but now we do our best work underwater. Besides, radar can tag you on the surface."

"Can't sonar see you underwater?"

"Only if you're good at it, sir." Casey exchanged a grin with Salli as she dialed commands into the computer. "And these guys ain't. We're closing them at a combined speed of twenty-two knots, and they got no idea we're here."

"How do you know?"

"Easy. A pirate sub—or another military's sub—isn't going to keep coming at a warship. That's how accidents happen. Accidents with torpedoes."

"Captain, I have positive I.D.," Salli said. "Computer profile has a seventy-five percent match to *Kilo* one-eight-two, owned by Vietnam." Her face twitched. "Profile matches Project 636 across the board, sir."

"Very well." Rothberg didn't frown, but Alex heard the disappointment in his voice. "Officer of the Deck, come left and open the range. There's no need to antagonize an ally."

"OOD, aye," Sue replied.

Paul glanced around the control room, his eyes narrowing as he turned back to Alex. "So that's it? We just go back to what we were doing?"

"Yep. We head for Victorie Station and we get back to work."

"Yeah. This life of yours is *super* exciting."

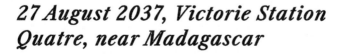

27 August 2037, Victorie Station Quatre, near Madagascar

Three days later, *Kansas* pulled into Victorie Station to investigate the pirate attacks. Immediately, they met resistance.

First off, the boat got stuck all the way out on a TRANSPLAT attached to Victorie Un, which was the dingiest of the seven hubs. Victorie's operations team told Alex there "was no undersea connection available" and relegated *Kansas* to an above-water TRANSportation PLATform. While it made for an easier time driving in, an inconveniently long elevator ride awaited every sailor who needed to get to or from the submarine from down below.

Also, since the pirate incident happened out in Victorie Quatre—Four—getting out there required a long boat ride with locals who didn't like them very much. Alex didn't speak a word of French, but he recognized at least one swear word, and he heard it multiple times while he and Paul were boated out to Victorie Quatre that morning.

Paul shrugged; ticked off locals were nothing new.

"Remind me to tell you sometime about the rental car and the pier in Rhodes," Alex said, mostly to pass the time.

"You mean that time you drove a fucking jeep off the end of a pier in SCUBA gear because it was fully insured, and the rental agency told you it covered absolutely *everything*?" Paul laughed. "Nancy told Janet, and she told me, you fucking legend."

"It seemed like a good idea at the time."

"One that might've gotten your ass kicked out of the Navy."

"Nah, a department head dared me to do it. Nobody wanted to take an admiral's son down with me." Alex grinned as the rundown platform for Victorie Quatre approached. Man, it was rusty. The fueling connections looked like they were in good shape, but the rest of the pier really needed a coat of paint to replace the seagull shit.

"Sometimes I wonder about your sanity."

"Says the guy who jumps out of planes and chases terrorists for a living."

Paul shook his head. "Gotta be safer than going to sea in a metal tube, dude."

"Pretty sure the death rate for parachutists is a shit ton higher than it is for submariners," Alex replied as the boat bumped up against the pier. "We're here."

"Thanks for the ride, man," Paul said to the boat's driver as they hopped out.

That earned them both a half-hearted glare from their guide, a young man who barely spoke three words since accepting their charter.

"Merci, Monsieur." He sped the boat away.

Scowling, Alex watched the rooster tail of spray kicked up by the boat. "That was mighty welcoming of him."

"Probably lumps us in with the terrorists. You note their fearless leader has a southern accent?" Paul asked.

"Someone should tell him the U.S. is a big country."

"Hell, you know as well as I do that people don't always care about that. 'Big Mean America' and all that."

"It's easier to hide from that shit on a submarine." Alex had encountered uneasy—or even angry—locals in many ports, though. Most times, people were welcoming of American dollars, if not American sailors. But some people didn't like the way a century of American policies shaped the world...and it showed.

"C'mon, let's get on with this so you can get back to hiding." Paul pulled Alex towards the elevator.

He threw up his hands in mock protest. "Why did I agree to come with you? Didn't they issue you Marines for this shit?"

"They're less fun to make fun of."

They stepped into the orange elevator, and Alex eyed the peeling paint while Paul punched in their destination. It lurched into motion with an ominous creak; Alex tried not to cringe.

He got stuck in an elevator during a snowstorm back at sub school. Surely that took longer than this.

Maybe.

They bantered their way down, mainly so Alex could ignore the sheer engineering failure this elevator represented and so Paul could pretend their destination wasn't near the bottom of the ocean. Victorie Station was deeper than Alderman's; Victorie Quatre sat in 600 feet of water, which made Paul twitchy.

So, Alex teased him about his disastrous Junior Ring Ball date with Nancy's roommate, Janet. That same Janet went on to marry the department head who dared Alex to drive a Jeep off the pier in Rhodes years later. Back then, Paul tried so damned hard to make everything perfect, wound up spilling red wine on Janet's blue dress—and his own white uniform trousers—and broke the box for his own class rings. He ended the evening by falling off a chair trying to sing along—badly—to a song by country singer Toby Keith.

Recounting that disaster took them all the way to the bottom, where they were met by the promised local guide.

"Commander Coleman and Colonel Swanson? I am Lydia North, the United Nations' Special Envoy for Undersea Matters," she said. "I am here to help with your investigation."

Lydia was a slender woman, with dark hair going gray and thick glasses that kept sliding down her nose. Unlike their ride in, she didn't look displeased to see them, more like a harried administrator who had one too many spinning plates to manage.

"Nice to meet you," Alex said, shaking her hand. Paul followed suit.

"I can show you where the pirates struck, but I'm afraid it won't be beneficial," Lydia said. Her British accent was noticeable when she spoke. "They burned up all the evidence. And most of the bodies."

Alex gulped back the need to puke. Going in that room was the *last* thing he wanted to do, but shit, that was the job.

He hung back and let Paul take the lead. Paul was—presumably—good with dead bodies. Alex chose his career in part so he could *avoid* them. Alex knew Paul did some shady shit as a Recon Marine. He must've spent plenty of time around dead people.

The stench hung in the room like a heavy curtain. Alex almost gagged when Emma led them in; the bodies were gone, but *damn* he could smell the burnt flesh. Charred outlines of the dead remained like an epitaph on the floor.

Damn, Paul didn't even flinch.

"This is one the station's main transfer facilities," Lydia said. "They brought a submarine up outside to transfer fuel out of the tanks"—she gestured at a bank of valves and gages—into their storage. You saw the video?"

"Yeah." Alex gulped back his nausea.

"They made a hell of a mess." Paul stared at the burnt floor, hands on his hips. "What's the point of terrorizing people? Couldn't they get what they wanted without a flame thrower?"

Lydia shrugged. "The crowd was unruly. I suppose they felt threatened."

"And bullets aren't such a great idea underwater." Alex examined the fuel transfer station. At least he knew what to do with *this*; the labels were in French, but valves were valves, even if the gages were in kilograms instead of gallons. "Poke a hole in the wrong thing down here, and everyone drowns."

"You're telling me that lighting things on fire is *safer?*" Paul gaped.

"Less likely to cause a leak, sure. Steel takes time to melt." Alex glanced at Lydia. "How much fuel did they get?"

"About forty thousand kilos," she replied.

Alex did some quick math. "That's about ten and a half thousand gallons. That's a lot of money." More math. "At current prices, that could net them, what, forty-thousand bucks?"

"A bit more than that, yes."

Paul frowned. "Isn't that a big tank to haul around on what you called a relatively small submarine?"

"You didn't hear?" Lydia asked. "They also stole a Neyk Three submersible with exterior fuel tanks to carry their haul away."

Further investigation proved worthless, only getting Alex and Paul heckled by locals. Lydia declined to translate what was said, even though they heard her speaking French with the station manager. That told Alex two things: it was ruder than rude and there was probably a lot of swearing.

"You know I speak Spanish," Paul said while they waited on the TRANSPLAT for their boat ride to show up. "I could understand enough of that to know it was vile."

Alex chuckled. "Get any good ideas from it?"

It was getting hotter, and the lack of shelter on the platform meant Alex felt every inch of his exposed skin burning. Thank goodness he was in civies and not a paper-thin uniform.

"Only that the locals don't like us much." Paul crossed his arms. "You know, I'm used to not being the popular kid—the Marines don't usually send me and my boys and girls places where we're going to be adored—but I thought the French were our friends?"

"Me, too. Must have missed that memo, or maybe it's just the folks out here." Alex shook his head. "It's double weird, since they seem frosty with Ms. North, too. The Brits and French are in bed together on all kinds of naval technology."

"Yeah? Their SpecOps guys don't like each other much."

That was new information, but the only special forces people Alex really knew were SEALs. And Paul. Yet the Brit and French submariners he encountered seemed amicable enough.

"Leaving so soon?" Lydia North approached from the dual elevator bank.

Alex shrugged. "You've done most of the work and sent us your data. There's not much else to do, other than try to find the, um, bastards before they strike again."

"I'll be glad to help with that, then." Her smile was smug. "I'll be coming with you. My superior just spoke to your captain, and it's been arranged."

"It has?" Alex exchanged a glance with Paul, who looked like he was trying not to laugh. "Well, I guess then you'll get to share our ride. Watch out, he's really friendly."

Chapter 4

Romance and Pizza

"**C**heck it out," Paul said a couple of hours later, wolfing down his fifth slice of pizza in the wardroom. It was pizza and wings night, always popular on the boat, and doubly so with the very bored Marines. "The media's got ahold of it."

"Oh, fucking joy." Alex sighed. "Let me guess—they're using clip art of Errol Flynn and romanticizing piracy?"

"No Errol Flynn, but apparently they call themselves the 'Deep Sea Devils.'"

"For fucks' sake." Alex almost spat out his red bug juice, the unidentifiable but popular fruit juice available on every submarine. "Really?"

Paul slid his tablet over so Alex could see the headline.

DEEP SEA DEVILS ATTACK UNDERSEA STATION

Erin Steeple, New York Times

27 August 2037—Four days ago, a group
of pirates calling themselves the "Deep
Sea Devils" attacked Victorie Station,
a majority-French owned station off
the coast of Madagascar. After killing
seventeen people and stealing over
10,000 gallons of gasoline, the pirates
evaded capture and remain at large.

The grisly video of their attack was
leaked online several hours after the
attack and has gone viral despite Victorie
Station administrators' attempts to take
it down. Seventeen grieving families
must now deal with the fallout of that
video—but who are these Deep Sea
Devils?

The Times received a message this
morning, purporting to be from the
group. They claimed credit for three
other thefts at other stations in the Indian
Ocean (Rihaakuru Underwater Towers,
Osborn Station, and Olhuveli Resort and
Mining Consortium, where they allegedly
kidnapped three major businessmen for

ransom). The Times was able to confirm theft of two civilian submarines from Osborn Station, but confirmations of any actions against the other two stations are still pending.

So far, the Deep Sea Devils have only communicated with the Times via email under a pseudonym. Facial recognition failed to identify any of them in the video from Victorie Station. However, we know they are led by a woman with an apparent southern accent.

If anyone has any information on these pirates, please contact the United Nations Undersea Emergency Office at undersea.emergency@unitednations.org or the Times at tips@nytimes.com.

"Well, that's a tin can of useless topped with some salty press opportunism, isn't it?" Alex rolled his eyes. "But it's real nice that someone told *us* these assholes apparently hit three other stations before they got here."

"Yeah, it explains the locals' hatred." Paul glared at what was left of his second serving of wings. "Aren't two of those stations right on top of this place?"

"All of 'em are pretty close." Alex sat back in his chair, stomach churning and appetite lost. "I wonder how many dead we're going to find from those three attacks?"

"At least a few." Paul's expression didn't change, which made Alex queasy. "I know the type, Alex. They're animals who don't value human life—they want what they want, and damn the consequences to everyone else." He bared his teeth. "Until the consequences come to get them."

"Consequences in the person of you."

"And my team, yeah. You get us there, and we'll take care of business. Once we find them, they won't be hurting anyone again. I can promise you that."

Kansas got underway from Victorie Station just in time for Lydia to hear that the pirates hit Agalega Farmstead.

"We got a video of that, too?" Alex asked as he, Paul, and Lydia settled into the wardroom to look at the evidence.

"Unfortunately, no. Just a report from the station keeper." Lydia flipped through several messages on her tablet. "She says that the pirates—who called themselves the 'Deep Sea Devils' and call their *Kilo*-class submarine *Golden Hind*—threatened to torpedo the farmstead if they didn't pay a ransom of thirty thousand euros."

"Torpedoes? Where the hell would they get torpedoes?" Alex frowned. "Broke dick old subs are cheap, but working torps are fucking expensive. Is there any evidence these fuckwits *have* torpedoes or was it an empty threat?"

"Better question," Paul said. "Why use the name of one of the most famous *privateer* ships in history? Are they working for some government?"

Lydia's perfectly sculpted eyebrows rose. "You know your history."

"I did a paper on Sir Francis Drake in college."

"I remember that." Alex resisted the urge to tell the story of how Paul selected said topic for their senior leadership paper just to piss off the executive officer of the Navy Department at Norwich University. Commander Bullerman was a prick—and a submariner, which meant he liked Alex. But he thought Paul was an arrogant meathead who'd go nowhere.

Paul turned in a meticulously researched paper that was four times longer than required to prove him wrong. It almost backfired when Bullerman tried to accuse Paul of plagiarism, because how could a rugby-playing numbnuts write something that good? Fortunately, Paul was proved innocent, and Bullerman wrote it off as a mistake.

Meanwhile, Alex's mediocre paper on Mush Morton sailed right up to an A-plus he probably didn't deserve.

"Fascinating," Lydia said in a tone that made it unclear if she was bored or thought it lovely that Paul knew some British history. "Moving on, you seem to be correct about the lack of torpedoes, Commander, despite your, uh, lovely language. When the station keeper called their bluff, the pirates—led by the same woman—forced their way onto the station and planted an improvised explosive device in an airlock. We do have video of that."

Lydia played video on the wardroom television. It was a little grainy, but it showed a team of four pirates attaching a homemade bomb to the inner door of an airlock. They were armed, two with flamethrowers, and two with what looked like knockoff AK-47s.

"I thought you said guns were a bad idea in a station, man," Paul said.

"They're still scary. Not that there's anyone to intimidate here." Alex glanced at Lydia and was met with a serene expression. "Did anyone talk to them in person?"

"No, it was all over the underwater telephone. Gertrude, I believe you call it?"

"Yeah."

"You're wondering how I know so much about submarines, aren't you? My older sister is a submariner. She's subjected me to too many tours over the years." A sigh. "This is *not* how I intended to spend my summer, but apparently, those skills come in useful."

"I hate to be that guy, but what happened to the IED?" Paul said. "Speaking of useful skills and all."

"Did they leave it there?" Alex gestured at the video, where the pirates retreated into the outer airlock and into their own submarine. *Golden Hind.* How pretentious.

"They did, and the station keeper paid the ransom." Lydia pushed her glasses up as they slid down her nose. "France is sending a team to defuse the device."

"France?" Alex and Paul asked simultaneously.

"Yes. Apparently one of their special forces teams was nearby in Mauritius for a training exercise." She pulled up a map on her tablet and cast it to the screen. "While Agalega Farmstead is right off the Agalega Islands and not too far north of Victorie Station, both the islands and the underwater farmstead owe allegiance to the government of Mauritius. Which, of course, has French roots."

"Of course." Alex tried not to scowl. Geography wasn't his strongest subject, particularly when it came to who owned which piddly island in the Indian Ocean.

Paul, however, was a world history nut who loved trivia. "France still has some colonies in the area, right?"

"Yes, Reunion and Tromelin Island are both in the area. There are others around Madagascar, as well. The French Navy has strong ties in the area, as do their marines."

"Of course they do. Everyone's carving out their slice of the pie out here. Going back to the pirates." Alex refused to call them by their stupid name. "What else happened?"

"Nothing. The station keeper paid up and they left like the civilized people they pretend to be." She checked her tablet. "Agalega's sensors tracked them moving northeast, but lord knows how long that lasted."

"Still, it's a start." Alex twisted to look at the navigation repeater screen on the bulkhead behind him. "There are two other big stations north of the Agalega Islands: Beach Loch and Quincy Mining Station, both owned majority-owned by the Seychelles."

"Great beaches. Better casinos." Paul grinned.

"Don't get me started about you and casinos." Alex rolled his eyes. "All right. In the absence of other information, we'll sprint and drift our way north, listening for *Kilos* or the Neyk Three they stole. You think that's still tagging along?"

Lydia shook her head. "There's a thriving black market for civilian submarines out here, particularly up off the coast of Somalia. Piracy may have dried up in *that* area, but the criminal element remains. There are a few stations out there that only deal in stolen goods, and God help you if you try to shut them down."

Paul's eyes lit up. "Sounds like fun."

"Easy there. I'll let you know when it's time to shoot someone."

"I do outrank you, you know." Paul flexed his muscles. "And when did *you* of all people start acting like an adult?"

"It had to happen to one of us when Nancy isn't around to keep us in line."

Master Gunnery Sargent Sarah Kochera was Paul Swanson's opposite in *every* way—excepting their sideways shared sense of humor.

"Now, Gunny, that wasn't very nice." Paul's voice barely hid his smile, and Alex saw laughter dancing in his eyes. "We both know how rowdy Marines get, but I understand that mascots are *important* on submarines, and these fine folks are our hosts. We should give the dog back."

"With all due respect, sir, it ain't just a dog." Master Chief Casey paused to shoot a glare at Kochera. "It's fucking *Toto*, and we need his ruby red slippers back, too, or you won't be in *Kansas* anymore."

Kochera groaned. "Really? You went there?"

"Gunny, you got no idea how low I'll go."

As an E-9, a Master Gunnery Sergeant was the equivalent of a navy Master Chief Petty Officer, which put Casey and Kochera on even footing. Excepting the fact that Casey—no giant, himself—was a good eight inches taller than Kochera. She was downright *tiny*, with dark hair, brown eyes, and a Napoleon complex that left Alex breathless.

Kochera was the senior enlisted member of Paul's team, one of the first female Recon Marines *ever.* And yeah, she was a nuclear missile on crack.

"Behave yourselves, children," Alex cut in. "I know that the whole Marine v. Sailor game is a time-honored tradition going back to the Revolution, but we *are* on the same side here."

"And I don't care how bored you are," Paul said. "Give them back their mascot, Gunny."

"Honest to God, Colonel, I don't have it."

"Yeah, and I'm the tooth fairy," Alex said. "You know who has it, so let's not split hairs. It might be a long underway, and guess what? Our cooks like Toto, too."

"Hey, messing with our food should be off limits, sir." Kochera's eyes narrowed. "It always is on the amphibs."

"That's the surface navy. Things are different on submarines."

"He's not pulling your leg, Gunny," Paul said. "I've known this guy for almost twenty years. You wouldn't *believe* the crazy shit he did back at Norwich."

"You're a Norwich guy, sir?" Kochera asked, cocking her head.

It went without saying that more Marines knew about Norwich than Navy types; Norwich University was the oldest private military school in the country. While most of the officers it commissioned went into the Army, there was a healthy smattering of Marines in every class. A strong handful went into the Navy, and fewer still into submarines.

"Some of us wear our muscles inside our brains," Alex replied.

Master Chief Casey made a choking sound that might have been a laugh. "You gonna get our damned mascot, Gunny, or do I have to get the captain to do an unannounced torpedo loading drill that coincidentally ruins all your shit? You friendly folks are sleeping in the torpedo room, after all."

Alex chuckled. "Oh, that's dirty."

"I aim to please, XO."

"Pony up the puppy, Gunny," Paul said. "I'll make it an order if you like."

"No need, sir." Kochera sighed. "Give me a sec to pry it out of DeToro's hands, and I'll be right back."

Alex wouldn't have thought such a tiny woman could *stomp* her way so vigorously through the hatch, but damn it if Kochera didn't. Yeah, he didn't really want to get on her bad side—he had a feeling Kochera knew fifteen ways to tie him into a knot without getting creative.

Which one was more dangerous? Alex didn't know. Paul might absently smash you into goo and apologize later. Kochera would probably kill you in your sleep.

Chapter 5

Striking Close to Home

29 August 2037, approximately 100 nautical miles southeast of the Seychelles

Kansas spent two days on a fruitless hunt in the vicinity of the Seychelles. A tropical paradise with gorgeous beaches and numerous resort casinos, they were one of the most popular vacation spots in the Indian Ocean—as well as a favorite liberty port for navy ships and submarines.

Kansas was scheduled for a visit in September for their upcoming change of command, where a new captain would take over from Commander Rothberg. Alex looked forward to some sun and good snorkeling—and maybe going to a casino like an idiot with Paul, assuming he was still on board—but he had mixed feelings about the change of command.

New captains were part of Navy life, but he'd miss Rothberg.

"I think I have a straight." Paul's brow scrunched up as he stared at the cards on the table between them in Alex's small stateroom. He sat in Alex's desk chair, making it creak in protest.

It was evening in *Kansas'* current time zone. With their search for the pirates moving westward, they'd have to advance another hour tomorrow. For now, however, the search was routine and boring, which left Alex with time to tackle the challenge of teaching his roommate cribbage.

"There's no such thing as a straight in cribbage, dude."

"Then whatever the fuck those four numbers are in a row. C'mon, can't you just tell me how many points it's worth?"

Alex stuck out his tongue. "You said you wanted to learn what submariners did in our free time."

"I figured you watched movies or jacked off. Who plays *cribbage* in the twenty-first century?" Paul sat back. "I give up. This is ridiculous. Too complicated by half and way too much math."

"Hey, I like math."

"Yeah, that says a lot about why you guys like this game."

"Cribbage is a sub tradition. The oldest boat in the fleet carries Dick O'Kane's cribbage board, and when that boat decommissions, they hand it on to the next oldest."

Paul rolled his eyes. "Is this where I'm supposed to know who—"

A sharp knock on the door cut him off. "It's open!"

Lieutenant Sue Grippo opened the door. The first thing Alex noticed was that Sue's hair was thrown into a much messier bun than usual, and there were circles under her eyes. "Flash traffic just came in, sir. Samar Station was attacked by the Deep Sea Devils."

"Samar?" Alex jumped off his rack so fast he almost hit his knees on the table. "When?"

"Two hours ago. Took them a bit to get comms back up—it sounds like they took a lot of damage and they're still counting the dead."

There wasn't much video from Samar Station, just news that got worse and worse while *Kansas* closed the range. What Lydia received from her contacts was brutal—an image of pirates connecting another improvised explosive device inside an airlock, and then another of the explosion.

The airlock camera itself died in the blast, as did the ones just on the inside of the hatch. Alex watched the interior station video a half dozen times, feeling sicker each time the wall of water rushed in on dozens of people as the alarms screamed. The feed always ended in static, and Samar Station's leadership didn't share much information beyond it—probably because they were still recovering bodies.

Kansas needed twenty-two hours to reach Samar Station. They used the old technique of sprinting and drifting to make sure they didn't miss the pirates *Kilo* on the way. Alex *hoped* they'd stumble on the bastards while rushing to the station's aid, but luck wasn't with them, and they arrived around dinnertime on 30 August.

Again, *Kansas* was relegated to a TRANSPLAT, but this time, no one minded. Samar Station was state-of-the-art; her TRANSPLATs were almost as big—though not as numerous—as those on the famous Armistice Station down south. Every piece of equipment was in top-notch condition, and the berth assigned to *Kansas* was right by the elevators. Samar was American owned, too, which meant security was tight and their welcome warm.

Or at least it should have been.

The pier was strangely quiet when Alex walked down the brow—the ramp connecting the deck of the submarine to the pier—with Paul. Normally, you'd see a couple of ships loading or unloading cargo and people moving about...but if there were more than a dozen people around, Alex couldn't see them.

"Feels like a murder scene," Paul whispered.

"You familiar with those?"

"Not *strictly* speaking, no."

"I am *not* going to ask for details about that." Alex shook his head. "Wonder where our husbanding agent is."

"You gonna stop speaking Navy and go back to English for us mere marines, or do I have to guess what that is?" Paul looked down into the water, frowning.

"Local who connects us with everything we need. Paid for by the Navy." Alex shoved his hands in the pockets of his Navy working uniform and wondered if he should have changed into civilian clothes like they had on Victorie Station.

Nah. Samar was American-owned, and being in uniform was more likely to get cooperation. He hoped.

"Good, you're already here." Lydia North breezed down the brow, waving her hands. "I've spoken to the station council, and they'll have someone meet us down on the terrace."

Paul cocked his head. "The Terrace?"

"The main floor. Or deck, as you navy types like to call it." Lydia sniffed and brushed past them. "Come along! We've work to do, gentlemen."

Alex grinned at Paul. "At least now we're gentlemen. Though I'm not sure about you, you uncivilized beast."

"Keep calling me that, and I *won't* have my boys and girls shoot these pirates when they come after you, Rook Brother." Paul's answering grin was all teeth.

"Sure you won't."

They had to rush to catch up to Lydia at the elevators—how *did* she move so fast in heels, and why in the world did she bring heels and a business suit to an *under*water station? Lord, this hurt Alex's head. Thank goodness the woman was smart, or he'd want to throw her overboard. Via a torpedo tube.

At least this elevator ride was free of ominous creaks and rusty hints at poor maintenance. Within minutes, the trio arrived on the main floor of Samar Mining Station. The mines themselves were on the ocean floor, but the bulk of Samar's business took place two decks above that on the Terrace. Built like a bubble-encased shopping mall, the Terrace was two decks of stores, restaurants, and every other necessity required by its rapidly growing population.

Samar Station sat off the west coast of the part of the British Indian Ocean Territory known as Diego Garcia. Britain's last possession in the Indian Ocean was nowadays leased by the United States and housed a Navy base mainly used supply ships and aircraft.

The Rush to the Ocean Floor, and the increase in multiple navies' presence in the Indian Ocean meant the base at Diego Garcia grew by a factor of five in just the last three years, but it was still small.

Not Samar Station. Samar Station sat on one of the world's biggest manganese deposits, which made the station founders *rich*. Manganese was one of the best oxidizing agents in the world. It was used commercially in rubber, glass making, fertilizers, batteries, and ceramics. But even more importantly, manganese was essential to steel production—and steel was needed for every underwater habitat.

Even better, Samar Station was located less than two miles off Horsburgh, in about 800 feet of water. That meant that the nearby naval forces on Diego Garcia were a significant deterrent to anyone who even thought about getting frisky—until now.

"Damn, this place is bigger than I thought," Paul said as they stepped out of the elevator.

"Samar Station has a population of twelve thousand people," Lydia said. "It's not the biggest underwater habitat—that trophy still goes to Armistice Station, followed by Azure Outpost in the South China Sea—but still sizeable."

"Impressive."

Alex had to agree. It was funny how a submariner had so little experience with underwater stations. Alex knew how to avoid driving into one and how to hook a submarine up to one—never much fun—but he hadn't spent much time at them.

"Bobbie would love this place," he said to Paul.

Paul chuckled. "Thinking of your next family vacation?"

"Maybe. Assuming Nancy and I can line our leave up right." Being married to another naval officer complicated things as they rose in rank. Alex was damned proud to say his wife outranked him—and that she would soon take command of her own destroyer—but damn, it got hard to do anything as a family.

"Nancy's too smart to want to spend her vacation underwater." Paul glanced up at the overhead dome and shivered. "It's pretty, but when I think about that giving way, particularly when a couple of ass nuggets popped explosives into this place, it gives me the creeps."

"Nancy likes novelties." Alex shrugged, his eyes tracing the dome. "And I don't see damage around here, so the IED must not have breached the primary dome."

Clearly their airlocks had multiple redundancies. Any undersea architect with half a brain would design things that way, but ten years' of undersea accidents said designers weren't always that bright.

"I take it you two are old friends?" Lydia asked as they passed a scuba gear shop Alex wished they had time to stop in.

"All the way back to the Wick, yeah," Paul said.

"The Wick?"

"College," Alex didn't have time to explain Norwich University's strange nickname before two people approached.

The taller of the pair was a woman with black hair and blue eyes. She had pale, angular features that made her look like she'd walked out of a teenager's vampire novel. The man was shorter and a portly. He was dark-skinned and fair-haired, wearing an impish smile that reminded Alex of a naughty child. But it was the woman who spoke.

"Welcome to Samar Station. My name is Ericka Ford; I'm a member of the Station Council. This is Tamar Becket, my colleague."

Tamar nodded. "Hello. I wish we were welcoming you during a better time, but it is good to have help."

"We'll do what we can," Alex promised. "I'm Lieutenant Commander Alex Coleman, Executive Officer, USS *Kansas*. This is Lieutenant Colonel Paul Swanson, commanding our Marine Detachment, and Ms. Lydia North, from the United Nations."

"Lady North, technically." Lydia waved a hand. "But that's unimportant. We spoke earlier, Ericka. I hoped you might show us the damage."

"Most of it's inaccessible but come this way, and I'll show you what we can," Ericka said.

She led them past a surprisingly large supermarket, a mechanics' shop, and a water purification plant. Then they ducked through a watertight hatch into a smaller hallway, one that lacked the transparent domed ceiling.

Here Alex could see water damage. There was running rust on two walls, and broken windows on multiple storefronts. Three doors were ripped off their hinges, several benches upended, and metal supports were bent. Repairs were in progress, but there was a lot left to do.

"As you can see, the watertight doors between this area and the next were open when the airlock was destroyed." Ericka's stone-like expression screamed her grief. "Everyone in this section of the station drowned."

Lydia's gulp was audible. "Don't you have automated safety features?"

"We do," Tamar said. "But they didn't account for a man-made explosion destroying both inner and outer airlock doors. The doors closed"—he pointed at the large metal doors at the end of the hallway—"but the area was already flooded and people were trapped inside. Our eductors couldn't dewater fast enough."

Alex swallowed. Imagining the onrushing wall of water was easy. Anyone in its path would only have had seconds before it hit them. The impact might've knocked the lucky ones out, but the less fortunate drowned as the space filled with water. There was nowhere to go. The watertight doors behind them were closed, and opening those would doom the rest of the station, thousands of other people.

"How many died?" Alex asked around the lump in his throat.

"Ninety-seven." Ericka's voice trembled.

"Damn," Paul whispered. "Hell of a way to go."

"Yeah."

Alex didn't mention that he sometimes dreamt of dying this way. Drowning or imploding were generally the submariner ways to go. Anyone who worked underwater accepted the risk of accidents happening. Yet the idea of *pirates* destroying an airlock to prove their mettle was unthinkable.

"We paid the ransom when they installed a second bomb, of course," Ericka said.

"A *second* bomb?" Paul spun around. "Is it still there?"

"No, they took it with them."

"That's a shame. My explosives gal could've told us a lot about them if they left it behind."

"Something tells me we're not going to be that lucky." Alex scrubbed his hand over his chin. "Did the pirates say anything when you passed the ransom to them?"

"Nothing. It was an electronic transaction." Tamar's shoulder's slumped. "You won't be able to help us much, will you?"

Paul shook his head, but Alex cut in. "That depends. Diego Garcia has some underground hydrophones out this way. If they got a good snapshot of what these guys' specific *Kilo* sounds like, we can track them."

"You want to say that in English?" Paul asked.

"Every individual submarine has a few specific tells when you listen to them on passive sonar. The older a boat is, the more unique it gets, because as you repair equipment, it starts to sound different. So, if these assholes got close to one of the hydrophone arrays—and they probably did—we should be able to dial them in. Then we can tell them apart from every other *Kilo*-class submarine in the world."

"I take it from your tone that there are a shit ton of them."

"From twelve different countries and whoever those countries sold them to, yeah," Alex said. "Five of those countries are in this part of the world, and the last thing we want to do is the nautical equivalent of pulling over the wrong guy. That's rude, and if the sub belongs to another navy, it could start a war."

Paul snorted. "The world's got enough problems without adding a war to the list."

Chapter 6

Hide and Seek

Senior Chief Sanelma Salli wasn't the most gifted sonar operator Alex ever worked with, but she was hard-working and conscientious. It took her less than an hour to pull up a comprehensive sonar profile on the pirates' submarine.

"I got 'em, sir. If we can hear them, we can track them," she said, gesturing at the waterfall sonar displays in *Kansas'* control room. "Sounds like their low pressure air compressor that *should* operate on the sixty-hertz line has a weird tick, and it's running at sixty-three hertz instead. They've also got a weird vibe back aft. The computer is ninety-nine percent positive it can differentiate this boat from every other *Kilo* submarine in the world."

"Great job, Senior Chief." Alex grinned.

"Black magic," Paul muttered.

Salli laughed. "Just good hydrophones and computer programming, Colonel."

"Witchcraft. Give me a gun and my own two eyeballs any day."

Alex cocked his head. "Weren't you just telling me about how you guys are integrating drones into Recon tactics?"

"I can control a drone with a *joystick*. Or my phone. None of this blind listening bullshit."

"Guess we know why you became a marine." Alex smirked.

"If that means it's up to your smart ass to find these fucknuts in this great big ocean, I'm fine with that," Paul said. "So, where do we start?"

"That's the complicated part. We can't hear everywhere, so we've still got to guess where they'll be and beat them there. And, as you said, it's a big ass ocean out there."

"Fan-fucking-tastic. So, more hurry up and wait."

"It's the name of the game."

2 September 2037, near Diego Garcia

"Still nothing on the search, Captain," Alex said as he ducked into Commander Rothberg's stateroom after three days searching for the pirates' submarine. "Even the new SOSUS lines near the base have nothing."

Rothberg sighed. "I wish I was surprised, but it's still early."

"That's going to be a shit explanation to the next station they hit." Alex slumped into a chair. "They're three for three without being stopped."

"And if they continue on pattern, we'll see a fourth hit in the next day or so," Rothberg said. "The politicians are going to have a field day with this. They like to forget that searching the ocean isn't like a cop waiting on the side of the highway for speeders."

"You want to deploy a couple of UUVs to expand our search box?" Alex asked, referring to Underwater Unmanned Vehicles.

Kansas had four UUVs, pronounced "You-Vees," tucked away in a back corner of her torpedo room. Most captains hated them and let the suckers gather dust. They took up space, reducing the sub's maximum capacity to twenty-one torpedoes instead of twenty-five, and were a general nuisance.

No one liked using them outside training, because the "high tech" unmanned vehicles liked to up and sink randomly. Sure, sometimes they extended your sonar picture. Sometimes, in perfect conditions, you could even use the onboard cameras to see things underwater. But usually the UUVs dropped like a rock to the ocean floor, never to rise again.

If you were lucky, and the water shallow enough, divers could pick them up like the marine equivalent of golf balls. Alex and *Kansas'* other rescue divers retrieved two of their UUVs during training off the coast of Key West, but no way was that an experience he cared to repeat. The fuckers were *heavy*.

Rothberg grimaced. "Probably the best plan. Pop a pair out and have them mow the lawn."

"Mow the lawn, aye." Referring to that search pattern always made Alex smile. "Maybe our lawnmowers won't sink today."

"Lord willing."

"You really do this boring shit for a living?" Paul asked eighteen hours later, squinting at the sonar screen over Senior Chief Salli's shoulder. He lost his fascination with sonar after about five minutes. Intellectually, Paul could understand how big the ocean was, but he wasn't good at waiting hours to get data.

The top display was what the Navy called a waterfall display. To the uninitiated, it looked like green squiggly lines on a screen, some fuzzier than others. Sonar operators, however, saw the sound gradient.

Old school sonar techs claimed all they needed was a waterfall display and a good set of headphones. However, the modern Navy also gave them a high-tech computer that synergized active and passive sonar inputs, calculating target motion analysis without old fashioned maneuvering boards and charts. That display was on the bottom monitor, right next to the currently-off video feed from the UUVs.

Toto, *Kansas'* stuffed terrier mascot—complete with his four custom-made ruby red slippers—was back in his designated home, nestled between the top waterfall display and the monitor to its left.

"Yep." Alex suppressed a smile.

Paul heaved a sigh. "No wonder why you people play cribbage. This'd drive me insane within a week."

"So, you're saying we're right on track?"

"Oh, fuck you." Paul's grin took any sting out of his words. "I'm so dragging you to the casino and winning *beaucoup* bucks off your ass the next time you're back in Connecticut, dude."

Alex laughed. "Says the guy who can't count cards."

Senior Chief Salli put her fingers in her ears and hummed. "You know they kick you out for that, sir."

"Only if you get caught." He grinned, and then elbowed Paul. "C'mon. You'll go crazy if we stand here any longer, and watching a sonar display doesn't make things happen any—"

"They've hit another station, Commander," Lydia North said as she walked into *Kansas'* control room, her lips pursed and features pinched. She was all business, and her scowl promised a storm.

"Shit." Alex wished he was surprised. "Where?"

"Weeper's Undertow. It's up by Lakshadweep," she added when Paul made a confused noise. "This time they indulged in blackmail as well as thievery—they bullied 'protection' money out of seventeen businesses and beat the snot out of four people when they objected."

Paul shifted slightly, the joker gone, his eyes hard. "Sounds like they need a date with my team."

"Anything else?" Alex asked. "Weeper's Undertow isn't busy enough to make protection money a good return."

"Right in one." Lydia grimaced. "The station does, however, have a brisk trade in civilian submarine repair, which allowed our dear 'Deep Sea Devils' to steal four civilian submarines."

"Four?" Paul reared back. "How the hell do you steal four submarines at the same time?"

"They have to have a mothership." Alex waved a hand, his mind racing. "Probably a surface ship, something with a well deck or a crane. Better question: what kind of boats did they steal?"

"Um." Lydia glanced down at her tablet. "One Triton 3700, a SDV-1200 Hybrid Submarine, a DeepFlight Super Falcon, and a Migaloo M4."

Alex whistled. "Damn."

"I presume that means something to you?"

"Yeah. That Migaloo costs megabucks. Millions, and not just one," he said. "Way better than that hypothetical casino win of yours, Paul."

Paul grimaced. "So they made bank."

"Quite," Lydia said. "Less blood this time, but more money. I fear they may have found their eventual operating model."

"Someone's got to notice when they try to sell those subs," Paul said.

Lydia shook her head. "Regretfully, no. There's a brisk black market for submarines in this part of the world. The only area worse is the South China Sea, and in nautical terms, that's practically next door."

"Great. So, we get to keep chasing them around the bad neighborhood, huh?" Paul slumped against the bulkhead.

"That's what they pay us for," a new voice said. Commander Rothberg smiled crookedly. "Pull in the UUVs and let's head to Weeper's Undertow, XO."

"Pull in the UUVs, aye." The response was automatic, but something nagged at him—Alex fought back a scowl.

Apparently without much success.

"Something wrong, XO?"

"I feel like we're playing a blindfolded game of hide and seek. We might have their sonar signature on file, but we'll never catch them this way." Alex shoved his hands in his pockets, chewing his lower lip. "We've got to break the paradigm somehow."

"Me and my peeps could pick a high value station to camp on and hope they show up. Might make a nice ambush," Paul suggested.

Rothberg shook his head. "That won't help if they threaten the station from a standoff distance or sneak an IED on board without you seeing them. You could die of explosive decompression, too, and then where would we be?"

Paul grimaced. "Pancaked."

"Your idea to use the UUVs is a good one, XO," Rothberg said. "If we fan them out as we approach, and we might catch something."

"Only if they leave on the same vector we're coming in on." Alex shook his head. "It's a big damned ocean, and they're playing us for fools. Unless the U.N. is going to cough up much bigger search party, or we get lucky, there's no point in playing their game."

Lydia shook her head. "I've asked for additional resources. Every nation says their ships and submarines are too busy to create a new task force."

Rothberg bristled. "When did you do that?"

"Yesterday." She met the captain's gaze. "It wasn't worth mentioning after they said no."

Rothberg's eyes narrowed.

Alex held up one finger. "Maybe Colonel Swanson's onto something. Maybe we ambush them."

"I thought that was a pancaking in the making," Paul said.

"Not if we bring them to us. We know what they want. It's not just blackmail or protection money; these guys are selling civilian subs on the black market. So, we bait them into picking up the boat *we* want them to—where we have some friendly neighborhood Marines waiting to greet them." Alex grinned. "And with *Kansas* nearby as backup, so they don't just sink the boat when they can't have it."

"That'd sure as shit ruin a perfectly good ambush, yeah," Paul said.

Rothberg scratched his chin. "That might work. Would the U.N. stretch to loaning us a high-end civilian submarine? Or renting one for us?"

"Preferably a Migaloo or a DeepFlight," Alex said. "They've already snatched up those, so we know they want them, and both sell for millions. Migaloos more so, particularly a M4 or M5."

Lydia frowned. "Perhaps. Are you certain this will work?"

"No." Alex laughed. "But it's got a lot higher chance of success than chasing these guys around like idiots."

She squared her shoulders. "Then I will go with you."

"What?" Alex felt like the deck dropped out from under his feet; he twisted to stare at Lydia. "You do know this is dangerous as hell, right? Like, bullets-in-the-face levels of dangerous. Not exactly the standard fare of Navy pirate chasing. We're going to let them catch *us*."

"And if I acquire you a submarine, Commander, it is *my* arse on the line if you lose it. So, I do think I will come along, if it's all the same to you."

"Are you sure about that?" Paul asked. "My team will try to keep you safe, but I can't guarantee anything in combat."

"Quite sure."

"Have it your way." Paul met Alex's eyes, and Alex read his worry. Would this crazy Brit ruin everything, or just get in the way? No way did they want a civilian along.

But the civilian was the money, so they were stuck with her.

6 September 2037, Samar Station, Indian Ocean

Three days of haggling later, Lydia North scared up a Migaloo M8—a sexier version of the super expensive civilian submarine the pirates stole from Weeper's Undertow. A submersible superyacht, the M8 was almost 500 feet long, had a top speed of fifteen knots submerged, and could carry up to 50 passengers and crew. It had Air Independent Propulsion, too, which was state of the art for a non-nuclear-powered submarine.

The M8 could stay submerged for up to four weeks and was big enough to carry two minisubs of its own. It was so expensive there wasn't even a list price online—Alex had to send Senior Chief Salli digging for one when he got curious. All she found was that the last M8 sold for more than $800 million.

"Yeah, this puppy will make a great payday for the Deep Sea Dipshits if they get their hands on it," Paul said.

They stood together on Samar Station's Number One TRANSPLAT, looking over the Migaloo M8 submarine. It was gray and white instead of the flat black Alex was used to, with windows—*windows!*—and a sleek outline, complete with inverse bow and tumblehome bow.

Alex scowled. "She looks more like a civil war ironclad than a submarine. Or a *Zumwalt*-class cruiser."

Paul laughed. "And here I was gonna say that she's pretty."

"Stick with your guns." He shoved his hands in his pockets, feeling weird to be out of uniform—but wearing a Navy uniform wouldn't exactly make him look like some civilian, would it?

Instead, Alex wore the plain coveralls favored by civilian mariners, as did the fifteen members of *Kansas'* crew accompanying him on this mission. Paul, on the other hand, was dressed like the rich owner who invited too many friends along for his joyride—and had too much stuff.

Crate after crate headed down the brow into the submarine, most labeled food, wine, or whiskey. Buried in with the goodies, disguised mostly as donuts and watermelons, were the marines' weapons. Their other gear was in boxes of spare parts and ice cream.

"You got all your 'friends' ready to go?" Alex asked as the last two crates went down the Migaloo's forward hatch.

"Ready to rock and roll, baby." Paul grinned, rolling his shoulders to show off how well his silk shirt fit. They *tried* to put him in a suit, but Samar Station didn't exactly stock suits for men built like tanks. Everything was either too wide in the waist or so narrow in the shoulders that one movement from Paul threatened to rip it in two.

"Then gather them up and we'll get underway within the hour." The one nice thing about civilian submarines was that they were designed to get moving a lot faster than a nuclear-powered boat like *Kansas*, and they needed way fewer people to run them.

"You sure you can drive this thing?" Paul's smile never wavered, in case they were being watched, but his tone turned serious. "I looked in the cockpit, and it looks nothing like what you're used to."

"All submarines operate on the same basic principles, and I *am* capable of reading the operator's manual." Alex rolled his eyes, not mentioning that he'd spent most of yesterday doing just that. Sure, he'd rather learn in a simulator, but the Migaloo was designed to be simpler than *Kansas*.

It wasn't like Alex was taking the civilian boat to war, anyway.

"All right, then. Don't stand here thinking too long." Punching him lightly on the shoulder, Paul winked and then headed over to his Marines, ushering his "party goers" onto the Migaloo.

Alex let out a long breath and then walked over to Commander Rothberg, who also stood on the TRANSPLAT pier about twenty feet away. Rothberg was also in civilian clothes—jeans and a worn out Chicago Bears t-shirt—just in case anyone was watching.

"Ready for your first command, Alex?" Rothberg grinned.

"I'm not sure this counts, sir."

"Maybe not officially, but experience is experience. And you're ready for command—not just of this mission, but of your own boat. I have every confidence in you."

"Um, thank you." He gulped. Knowing that Rothberg liked and respected him was one thing—this unsolicited compliment made him want to stutter.

"Don't thank me. This is your crazy plan." Rothberg laughed. "I look forward to seeing how it works out."

"Gee, that's a great vote of confidence."

"I'll try not to let you get captured by pirates."

Damn, that was a sobering thought. Being stuck in a civilian submarine with twenty-one marines and fifteen sailors was already an oil-and-water combination, but if the pirates had their way, it might all go up like a tinder box.

Nope, Alex had to trust Paul to take care of business when the chips fell.

"Try not to follow too closely, sir," he said. "We don't want to scare them off."

"The day a creaky old *Kilo* can hear *Kansas* is the day I go shopping for a new career," Rothberg replied. "You sure you don't want to kick Lady North off? I'm sure the U.N. will get over her absence, and it's hard to vouch for her safety on board."

"The lady's got the money, and she's hard to ignore."

"I'm only joking. Besides, I already tried to talk her out of it and failed." Rothberg offered him a hand. "Fair winds and following seas, Alex."

"Same to you, Captain."

Alex headed for the Migaloo and didn't look back.

Chapter 7

Party Time

"**W**e need to name this bucket," Paul said eight hours later, playing a game on the high-end tablet that came with the submarine.

The Migaloo was well clear of Samar Station and headed northwest, roughly in the direction of Weeper's Undertow. Chugging along at a mere ten knots, the civilian submarine wouldn't get anywhere fast, but Alex wasn't concerned with speed.

He *was* concerned that the party-boat vibe Paul's marines had going back aft—complete with loud music and a set of drums someone snuck on board—would give him a headache. The noise was good since they wanted to be heard...but his teenaged daughters were better behaved.

Alex grimaced. "I veto whatever it is you're thinking of. Twice."

"C'mon, you act like I'm going to suggest *Chesty Puller* or *Yellow Submarine*." Paul twisted in his chair to put his feet up on the console.

Alex watched but didn't comment; Paul wasn't dumb enough to put his size fourteen shoes on something sensitive. Instead, he turned to Senior

Chief Salli, who monitored the Migaloo's sensor array from the leftmost seat.

"What do you think, Senior? Should we name this sweet little boat after a marine no one other than jarheads remember these days?"

"Sir, I'd rather take a walk topside. While submerged." Salli never took her eyes off the console, but Alex saw her smile.

"See?" He cocked his head at Paul. "You're outvoted."

"Pah. You squids have no sense of humor. How about *Ranger?*"

Salli frowned. "After the aircraft carrier?"

"Better than the army type," Alex said.

"Am I the only one with an appreciation for history?" Paul shoved a candy bar into his mouth. "No, *I* was suggesting *Ranger* for Captain Benjamin Hornigold's ship. He was only one of the most famous pirate hunters of all time. Though I suppose you could *also* reference John Paul Jones' ship from the early days of the Revolutionary War."

Alex snorted. "Nerd."

"That's actually kind of cool, sir," Salli said.

"Oh, now you're a traitor, Senior? I see how it is. You were supposed to back me up against the jarhead."

Salli's grin was lazy. "I'm not sure *which* interaction of ours ever gave you that idea, sir."

A few hours later, Lieutenant Sue Grippo relieved Alex in the "cockpit." Why the civilians named a perfectly good control room after something that belonged in an aircraft, Alex didn't know, but he itched to tear the annoyingly bold-lettered sign on the door down. Instead, he took a walk.

Familiarizing himself with the Migaloo—*Ranger,* he supposed—was harder than expected. Driving it was easy; a submarine was a submarine once you figured out the controls. But the high-tech luxury unnerved him.

Everything was *pretty.* Shiny, he could understand; polished metal didn't rust or corrode. But artwork? Plush lounge chairs, giant windows, and two mosaic-covered jacuzzies? Compared to *Kansas'* utilitarian lines, with equipment and weapons shoved in every available corner, the Migaloo was another planet.

Paul, oddly, was in his element. Alex never realized what a chameleon his old friend was—maybe that was the special forces thing. Paul's spoiled rich guy persona hit every note and played it loud; he organized fake parties, loud music, and endless food buffets. The marines and Alex's off duty *Kansas* sailors drank non-alcoholic beer and pretended to be drunk, singing karaoke and hoping the pirates' *Kilo* would pick up the sounds of partying.

Someone howling out the lyrics to The Sideways' latest hit made Alex cringe. Any sonar operator with a set of ears within twenty miles would hear that—better, if bottom bounce conditions were good.

You want to be heard, you fool, he reminded himself for the fortieth time. *Letting* someone find his submarine went against fifteen years of training. Alex shuddered.

"See a ghost, sir?" Gunny Kochera asked from behind him.

Alex jumped. "Not until you showed up. But you might've just killed me from fright."

"No way. That's boring." She grinned, all teeth. "I can think of *way* better ways to kill people. Much more fun for everyone."

"I'm...not going to ask about that."

"Hey, you brought me along to kill pirates, sir." Kochera twirled like a vicious ballerina. "Don't be sad because I'm good at my job."

"*Sad* is not the word I'd use. What *are* you doing, anyway? I thought you'd be enjoying the party back aft."

"I'll join them when I'm done setting up operation scavenger hunt," she replied, gesturing at the trunk on the deck behind her. "Colonel wants us to hide weapons in all kinds of useful places, and I'm the most creative."

"Now *that* I never doubted." Alex eyed the crate. "You guys are using rubber bullets, right? Poking holes in the pressure hull is a really shit idea."

"We got the lecture already, Commander." Her smile was more natural. *Finally.* "Probably word for word what you told the Colonel. 'Don't bust holes in the people space.'"

"Pretty much, yeah."

"No sweat. We don't want to die down here, either. I'm okay with arranging for a couple of pirates to meet their maker, but I'm not going down in an underwater coffin. No matter how luxurious."

Alex grinned. "Now that's something we can agree on, Gunny."

9 September 2037, in the northwest Indian Ocean

"Scope's clear," Alex said as *Ranger's* periscope broke through the waves three days after they left Samar Station.

He kept his hands steady on the controls, enjoying being able to drive the submarine. Enlisted sailors got to have all the fun driving warships, but the Migaloo was designed to run mostly by computer—except during critical operations like surfacing and diving.

This one-man operation was so different from what he was used to. Like *Kansas*, the Migaloo had a camera array instead of a traditional periscope you put your eye up against; the display for it was on Alex's left. Advanced attack submarines needed multiple people to bring them to the surface. But *Ranger* had automated ballast controls, and from what Alex could tell, they worked pretty well.

"Surfaced."

It was a pity the Navy couldn't figure out how to automate more systems. Alex supposed civilians didn't have to worry about battle damage.

"I still don't understand why this is necessary." Lydia crossed her arms, standing framed by the cockpit hatch. Trying to tell her to sit down was pointless, particularly because the four seats in the cockpit were filled with Alex, Paul, Sue Grippo, and Senior Chief Salli.

"Two and a half days of putzing about hasn't gotten us spotted." Alex shrugged. "We'll make more noise on the surface, particularly if the Marines have their way."

"Oh, we will." Paul grinned. "Gunny's got some special dance moves planned."

Alex laughed. "I'm so not asking about that."

"Yeah, probably better that you don't."

Lydia cleared her throat. "And we assume that this adolescent display will get us the *desired* attention?"

"Beats chugging around down here with the whales." Alex dialed in a course and flipped the autopilot switch to on. "And if they *do* have a mothership—which they pretty much have to—they're a whole lot more likely to spot us on the surface. This boat's not the quietest submarine in the water by a large margin, but surface ship sonar sucks. Particularly on civilian ships."

"If they even have it," Sue added.

"And there's that."

Lydia huffed. "And what do we do if their *submarine* approaches? Correct me if I'm wrong, but isn't catching that quarry the entire point of this operation?"

"*Kansas* is still shadowing us, ma'am." Sue's expression was carefully blank. "She's made for this. No way will they hear *her*, particularly with us making noise up here."

"If you say so, Lieutenant."

Yeah, Sue's smile was strained. Alex made a mental note to ask her about her beef with Lydia when they were alone. Something was wrong here.

"All right," Alex said. "We're stable on the surface and I'm swapping to surface navigation. Someone needs to stay on watch in here at all times, but batteries release on the party topside."

Paul grinned. "On it."

He vanished through the hatch with boyish glee. Lydia trailed on his heels, shaking her head like a disapproving school master.

"You might as well take your hair down, Sue." He flipped the autopilot on for a leisurely speed of five knots to nowhere and made a show of putting his feet up. "We're not supposed to look Navy. I'd say the same thing to Senior Salli, but her hair's shorter than mine."

Salli laughed. "Not my fault your hair's barely in regs, sir."

"Hey, close counts in horseshoes, hand grenades, and haircuts."

Sue fidgeted. "This doesn't feel...weird to you, sir?"

"Which part? Swanning about in wacko civilian luxury and waiting for pirates to attack us? Or is it the marines grinding like horny teenagers back aft?" Alex laughed. "Seems perfectly normal to me."

"If you say so, XO."

Alex pulled his feet down and sat up straight, turning to face Sue. "Time to spill the beans, Nav. What's bothering you?"

"I'm just not sure this is what I signed up for. *Kansas* is doing what attack subs are supposed to do—hunting bad guys, dropping off special forces, maybe doing a little spying." Sue bit her lip. "But being bait while *Kansas* probably gets to shoot the pirates? I know it's necessary, but it feels, I don't know, wrong. We didn't train to be bait. We trained to take the fight to the enemy."

"And hunting pirates is every naval officer's job."

"Yeah."

"Well, I could lie and tell you that there's nothing out of the ordinary going on, but one look at this palatial cockpit would prove me wrong," Alex said.

"So, yeah, it's a bit weird. But we *are* doing our job, even if it's from a civilian submarine. And this kind of thing has deep roots in naval history, with disguised merchant ships being to suck in enemies going all the way back to the seventeenth century."

"So, you're saying that while *we* might be crazy, history will say it's normal."

"As far as I know, no one's ever done it with a submarine before. We get to be first with that."

"Oh, that makes me feel *so* much better, sir."

Alex didn't mention that the victims of historical "Q-Ships" were generally submarines, particularly during the First World War. Paul was the all-around history nerd, but Alex enjoyed naval history. He dug back into the subject after coming up with this crazy idea.

Q-Ships had limited success in wartime, despite being responsible for ten percent of U-Boat sinkings in World War I. Once the enemy caught on, they kept their distance and sank anything suspicious looking. But this wasn't a war. The Deep Sea Pirates weren't interested in *sinking* anyone—they wanted money, and to get the big bucks, you had to steal and sell the submarine. Hard to do that if it was on the bottom.

Harder still to do it if the boat was full of marines burning to mess your day up.

"Fishing, dude? Really?"

Paul joined Alex on *Ranger's* forward deck. He towered over where Alex sat, fishing pole in hand and far enough from the boisterous party back aft that he could pretend it wasn't happening. Migaloo Submarine called the main deck of their submarines the "beach deck," and the boats were designed for surface entertainment almost as much as underwater. One deck up was the "sun deck," with two hot tubs, lounge chairs, and a helo landing pad for the super-rich—which they weren't. So, the marines set up a volleyball net and a barbeque, as well as using the surprisingly good waterproof topside speakers.

Alex enjoyed sunbathing, water, and beaches as much as the next guy, but he preferred swimming to loud music and dancing. That led him forward to *Ranger's* bow and a deck down, which wasn't designed for partying—but was a good place to sit and fish. Sue had the watch for the next three hours, and Alex meant to enjoy the sunset.

"Beats your marines' 'steel beach' volleyball." Alex gestured aft and up, where a vicious five-on-five volleyball tournament waged. "Someone's going to break their face diving for a ball."

"Hey, they're fit, not stupid." Paul plopped down next to him. Like the marines, Paul was clad only in a bathing suit and his many tattoos—few of which, Alex suspected, were permitted by USMC regulations. *Special rules, special forces.* "I trust them not to hurt themselves too much."

"It'd be a real shame to get taken over by pirates because our fearless protectors all smashed themselves to bits playing with a ball."

"You really have to worry about your sailors that much?" Paul laughed. "Marines know better than to—"

Klonk.

"Oh, shit, Fernandez—" someone shouted.

Splash.

Alex's head snapped around.

A marine slid off the top deck, bounced off the beach deck with a sickening *squish*, and tumbled right into the water. Like most civilian submarines, Migaloos had life rails to use on the surface, but they didn't go all the way aft because of the helo pad, and the marine fell far enough back to avoid every safety feature.

Alex's right hand jerked his radio up on its own. "Nav, XO, man overboard, man overboard, starboard side! I say again, man overboard, starboard side!"

"Fuck!" Paul raced aft, with Alex on his heels, fishing pole forgotten. Running on a steel deck—even one with artificial, non-skid, footing—was a challenge in flip flops, but it wasn't like he had time to change.

Ranger heeled outboard as Sue threw the sub into a starboard turn. Paul stumbled for balance, but Alex darted past him, his eyes on the water where Fernandez went overboard. Seconds counted down in Alex's head as the stern swung to port, away from where Fernandez should pop up—

"There he is!" one of the other marines shouted just as Alex reached the end of the beach deck.

Fernandez bobbed to the surface, face half down and bleeding from the head.

Shit.

Paul skidded to a stop right behind him. "Nowak, Toney, you two are our strongest swimmers. Get your asses down here!"

"Those two rescue swimmers?" Alex asked.

"No, but—"

"Then no buts," he cut his friend off, raising his radio again. "Nav, XO, man bears zero-nine-five relative, range approximately fifty yards."

"If you think we've got time to wait with Fernandez face down out there, you are *crazy*," Paul hissed in an undertone.

"No, I think the ocean will eat your marines alive, particularly without fins, and I'm not up to rescuing *three* people today." Alex shoved the radio into Paul's hands. "Keep giving Nav relative bearings and estimated distances. She's probably got him on camera by now, but live eyes have better depth perception. And throw me a fucking life ring when I get close enough, because swimming in open ocean without fins sucks."

Alex chucked his flip flops off and dove into the water before Paul stop him.

Damn, it was slow going. The water was around eighty degrees, so the lack of a wet suit wasn't an immediate problem, but swimming in a t-shirt and board shorts wasn't Alex's thing. He was used to doing this in a wetsuit, with fins, a mask, and a snorkel. And he *hated* getting salt water in his eyes.

But Alex hadn't qualified as a rescue diver without being a strong swimmer, and the current was with him. He settled into a good pace right away, hampered only by the need to check Fernandez' location with every breath he took. Luckily, Fernandez landed only half face down, which meant he wasn't *completely* drowning when Alex reached him.

Still, Alex wasted no time flipping the marine on his back and doing a quick pulse check. Yeah, Fernandez's pulse was thready, but there—but his breathing was touch and go.

No way to fix that in the water.

Treading water, Alex looked to see where *Ranger* was. The Migaloo was mid-circle, coming back around in a standard man overboard maneuver towards where Alex held Fernandez's head and shoulders above the water. Fortunately, the sea was calm... for the tail end of monsoon season.

Judging angles and distances, Alex started towing Fernandez to where he figured Sue would stop *Ranger.* Swimming all the way back to the boat was stupid, but training said she'd meet him halfway. That meant another few hundred yards' swim, which wouldn't be too bad with fins, even with two-to-four-foot waves. Hauling a marine twice Alex's weight without them was much harder.

His muscles burned with fatigue in minutes. Alex concentrated on counting strokes and keeping his rhythm steady and strong. Speed was not paramount; the sub could move faster than him, and rushing could get them both dead.

A splash hit the water a few feet to Alex's right. He grabbed for the life ring without looking, hooking his free arm inside it and holding on tight.

"Pull!" Paul's shout carried across the water.

The marines hauled in on the line, carrying them the last twenty-five feet. By then, some of the *Kansas* sailors had a dive ladder rigged over the side and a rescue basket waiting in the water.

Using the last of his energy, Alex heaved Fernandez into the metal litter and strapped him in. Usually, that was a two-swimmer job, but both of *Kansas'* normal rescue divers remained on the boat, so he ignored his knotting muscles and got the job done. On Senior Chief Salli's command, the *Kansas* sailors hauled the litter up on deck, and Petty Officer Klusky—the corpsman attached to Paul's unit, since the USMC borrowed their medics from the Navy—started CPR.

Hauling himself up the ladder felt like a herculean task, but it beat treading water, so Alex forced himself up to the beach deck and flopped into a sitting position. Once he stopped moving, his legs hurt less.

"Nav, Swanson, all on board," Paul said on the radio. Alex barely heard him over the pounding of his own heart.

He'd acted without much thought, just done what needed to be done, but in hindsight, jumping off the deck of his first command—temporary or not—probably wasn't the best idea. But it wasn't like they brought another rescue swimmer along. Regulations required both of *Kansas'* two official swimmers to stay on the boat. Alex, like any qualified officer, was an off-the-books bonus. He maintained his qualifications for fun.

No one really cared if the borrowed civilian submarine had a rescue swimmer, a fact that just almost cost Fernandez his life.

"Damn, that's harder without fins."

"You're fucking crazy, you know that?" Paul loomed over him.

Alex arched and eyebrow, peering up at him. "I'm the only qualified rescue swimmer on this boat. What the fuck did you *think* was going to happen?"

"Rescue swimmer? I knew you liked diving and all, but that's a thing? And your thing?"

"Subs get underway. People fall overboard sometimes. We like to be able to get them back. Drowning's bad for morale." Alex chuckled. "But we kind of like to plan things better, like having a swimmer standing by with fins and a wetsuit and all that good stuff."

"You know what they say about plans." Paul grinned and offered him a hand, pulling Alex to his feet like he weighed nothing.

"I'll make a note to consider volleyball the enemy next time, yeah." Alex turned to where Klusky remained bent over a semi-conscious Sergeant Fernandez. "How's he looking?"

"Breathing and stable, sir. Best I can do for now."

"All right." Alex took a deep breath and glanced around at the worried faces of both sailors and marines. "I think we've had enough time topside for the moment. Let's stow the party supplies and get ready to dive."

"Aye, sir," most of the group murmured.

"Good call," Paul said quietly. "Thanks, by the way. You saved Fernandez's life. I didn't expect you to go jumping in after him."

"Better me than you. You'd probably sink like a rock, and hauling your ass back would've been even less fun." Alex felt even smaller next to Paul right now, dripping wet and growing colder.

Paul barked out a laugh. "Yeah, that'd suck for both of us."

"More for you. I'd knock your ass out with an elbow to the face, first."

"Bullshit."

"Nope. That's one of the first tricks they teach us to deal with unruly rescues. But for you, I'd make it a special gift."

Chapter 8

Bait

"That was a very brave thing you did," Lydia North said from the cockpit doorway.

Alex twisted in his seat, aching muscles screaming. "I'm the only rescue swimmer on board. I wasn't about to let him drown. Though next time, I'd really rather do it in a wet suit and fins."

"Do officers usually train as rescue swimmers in the U.S. Navy?" Lydia pursed her lips. "My understanding is that it isn't normal in the U.K."

Alex shrugged. "Not usually. But my first boat had a hard time getting an enlisted sailor through the course, so I volunteered. I've kept my quals up ever since. It's not hard since I'm a recreational diver."

"Interesting." She blinked a few times, like she wanted to fidget and wouldn't.

"Everything all right?"

"Yes, fine." Lydia's smile didn't reach her eyes. "I simply assumed this mission would be faster. My superiors are not happy."

He chuckled. "They're not really sub hunters, are they?"

"No, politicians tend not to be."

"I'm not really acquainted with the breed, to be honest. Never really wanted to be." Alex was Navy through-and-through. The first in his family to graduate college, he scraped in on a NROTC scholarship and then got into submarines through decent grades and hard work.

Politics were something he didn't like and didn't want to understand. His older brother, Sam, sometimes told him about the politicking inherent in being a state policeman. It made Alex's head hurt. Even Navy-style politics didn't really start to get you until you made captain, or O-6, and that was as far as Alex's ambition went. He wanted command of a submarine—two, if he could get it—but someone else could be an admiral.

Maybe his wife would do that. Commander *Nancy* Coleman was high speed, smart, ambitious, and the love of his life. She was at the Surface Warfare Officer's Prospective Commanding Officer course right now. Soon, she'd embark on her first command, a shiny new *O'Bannon*-class destroyer. Nancy was usually one step ahead of Alex in their career progression, and he'd love to see her wearing stars.

Provided she dealt with the politicians and he never had to.

"Going into politics is a time-honored tradition in my family." Lydia's smile was wan. "I wanted to be a nurse, but when my older sister stayed in the Royal Navy, the duty fell to me. Our father still thinks she'll 'come to her bloody senses,' someday."

Alex laughed. "I think I'd like your sister."

She cocked her head. "Perhaps you would." Lydia cleared her throat. "However, I didn't come forward to discuss Ursula. As I said, my background is in nursing. I understand that Petty Officer Klusky is taking care of Sergeant Fernandez. I would like to offer my help."

"That's very kind of you." And a damned good idea, Alex couldn't say out loud. Klusky seemed like a good corspman, but he needed to sleep, and nobody else had medical training beyond that of a first responder. Alex probably had the most from his rescue swimmer training, but he couldn't afford to get stuck playing nurse. "We'd be very grateful if you're willing to help."

"Shall I head back aft, then?"

"Please. I'll let Colonel Swanson know."

Eleven hours of putt-putting around underwater later, the phone in Alex's cabin rang. He couldn't call the place a stateroom—it was *way* too plush for that, complete with a fluffy queen-sized bed that was too soft, a stereo system that could make his teenaged daughters jealous, and three large screen televisions showing the Migaloo's exterior camera views. The view was gorgeous, at least when they were shallow enough for light to filter down, but having windows in a submarine was just *weird*.

Still, a long swim was always a great excuse for a nap, particularly after several hours on watch. By the time Alex finished his six hours in the cockpit, he was bone-tired and his muscles alternating between aching and burning, so he ignored the too-soft mattress and passed out.

He got three hours of sleep before the phone belting out the tune of something Mozart woke him up. It took three tries before Alex found the speaker button—there were no handsets on this luxury craft, oh, no. Just headsets and speakers.

"XO." He squinted at the clock before giving up. The dull pounding in his head told him *too much salt water, not enough sleep*. That was all he needed to know.

"Sir, it's the Navigator. I think they found us."

Alex sat up so fast his back cracked. "Bingo. I'm on my way."

Throwing on his all-too-civilian coveralls, Alex bolted for the cockpit, where Sue sat in the pilot's seat, her eyes riveted on the sonar display. Two seconds on this overpriced boat taught the Navy crew that Migaloo-brand sonar was crap, but there it was, plain as day: another submarine about two miles aft of them.

Senior Chief Salli arrived right on his heels, slipping into the sensor operator's seat without a word. That left Sue in the driver's seat, with the captain's chair open for Alex. He didn't sit down.

"They've been creeping up on us slowly over the last couple hours, sir," Sue said. "They probably don't think we've seen them, but they're so close that it's *got* to be our guys. Anything else is just bad manners."

"Yeah, they're pretty much asking us out on a date right now." Alex frowned at the plot. "They say anything?"

Sue shook her head. "Nope."

"*Rude* is the right word." Alex smiled wryly. "I'm going to guess that contact up there is their mothership, huh?"

"Definitely a surface ship moving at slow speed, sir." Senior Chief Salli frowned at her display. "The sonar library here doesn't have military profiles in it, but it's a single screw diesel, paralleling our course. If I had to guess, I'd say it's an old amphibious ship some Navy or another sold off. Maybe Russian, maybe ours. Either way, it'll have a well deck where they can hide the subs they steal."

"Even ones this size?" Sue asked.

"Might be a big fucking well deck." Alex chewed his lip for a moment before deciding that he could worry about that later. "Let's wake up the marines and then try talking to these guys."

"Way ahead of you, Rook Buddy." Paul's voice came from the still-open hatch, but his grin was ruined by a yawn.

"Oh good, now that Sleeping Beauty is here, we can get to work." Alex winked at Sue, who snickered. "Your team ready to rock and roll, Paul?"

"We will be long before those yahoos can get over here."

"Then let's rig the trap. Remember, you're an offended rich dude until *Kansas* can bag their mothership, too."

"Be an affronted millionaire, aye." Paul slapped Alex on the shoulder. "Be careful up here. These assholes have proven willing to kill people who piss them off, so don't add yourselves to the list."

Sue's sharp intake of breath made it hard not to twitch. Alex grimaced.

"We'll try not to. Get your ass in gear."

One nod, and Paul was gone, leaving Alex, Sue, and Senior Chief Salli alone. This crazy plan of his suddenly felt *real*—and insane. Who was he to go fishing for pirates...as the bait?

But they'd found the pirates. Surely that counted for something. Hunting pirates was every naval officer's duty, and these 'Deep Sea Devils' weren't just people who stole ships for ransom. They'd killed people, innocent people, and for what?

"You want to drive, sir?" Sue's voice was tiny.

"Nah, but I'll do the talking." Alex couldn't believe he was volunteering for this—he *hated* public speaking, but with his heart racing and mind focused, the idea of getting on the radio wasn't as awful as usual.

"You feeling okay, XO?" Sue asked. "Everybody on the boat knows how much you love attention."

Alex shrugged. "I just want to get on with this." Bracing himself, he picked up the handset for the Gertrude, or underwater telephone.

A Gertrude was the only reliable way to talk from submarine to submarine, and it wasn't long-ranged. U.S. Navy submarines—and expensive civilian ones, like this Migaloo—had communications wires that they could "stream" towards the surface to communicate with ships and aircraft above water. However, unless there was someone up there to relay, the best way to talk to someone else *under*water was a Gertrude. Technology just hadn't gotten to the point of having easy and clear underwater communications. Not yet.

Alex licked his lips. "Hey, uh, submarine near..." He hesitated a touch too long before reading off the latitude and longitude, trying come across like a civilian mariner who didn't rattle these things off in a military cadence. "You're closing in on my position pretty quickly. Can I help you, over?"

The response was immediate, from a woman whose southern drawl did not hide the edge in her voice: "Migaloo M8 submarine, this is the *Golden Hind*. You are being commandeered. Surface and prepare to be boarded, or we will torpedo you, over."

"Torpedo?" Sue's jaw dropped. "I thought intel said they didn't have torpedoes?"

Alex made sure the radio wasn't transmitting before replying: "I'm sure they don't, but we're scared civvies who don't know that. So, let's just be scared, yeah?"

"I'm more scared of them ramming us, sir." She gestured at the radar plot, where the "unknown" submarine continued inching closer.

"Yeah, that's looking pretty fucking intimate." Alex chuckled. "You think I waited long enough for them to assume we're freaking out over here?"

"Probably."

Clearing his throat, Alex lifted the radio microphone again. "Did you say *torpedoes?* We—we don't want any of that."

"Then surface immediately. Over."

"Ooh, they sound pissed." Alex didn't want to say he was enjoying himself, but man, thinking of the surprise waiting for these assholes was kind of nice.

Sue chewed her lip. "Might be time to listen, sir."

"Yep. Let's do it." Alex slid into the captain's seat to punch in the correct commands on the dive control panel, easing *Ranger* towards the surface. He keyed the radio again. "*Golden Hind*, this is *Ranger*. Surfacing now. Please don't shoot, over."

"We won't if you hurry," *Golden Hind* replied.

The utter lack of compassion in that voice made even Alex shiver a little, and his hands wanted to shake when he thumbed the transmitter off. Swapping to interior communications, he keyed the intra-sub intercom: "All hands stand by for surfacing. Expect visitors soon thereafter."

"Better strap in, sir," Senior Chief Salli said.

"Not a bad idea." Grimacing, Alex matched actions to words and buckled his seatbelt.

"One hundred feet and rising," Sue said. "Want to slow down and make it gentle, sir?"

"Nope." Alex goosed the ballast controls, rocketing the sub upwards.

Ranger's nose breached the surface first, going a hair too fast—ten knots—and then slammed down with enough force to slam all three sailors forward in their seats. They wheezed as their seatbelts jammed into their stomachs. The rest of the sub burst up in a great wave, rocking port to starboard and back again like a drunken whale. Alex's back cracked with the impact, and Sue swore as she struggled to keep the boat under control.

Salli hissed. "Jesus, sir."

"You think they're convinced it's amateur hour?" Alex grinned.

"Shit, XO, *I'm* convinced." Salli scowled. "I almost pity the marines back aft."

Alex unbuckled his seatbelt and rose. "They're young and fit. They'll be fine. Pull up the cameras, will you, Sue?"

"Cameras, aye." Sue cast the deck camera views—there were three of them—onto the top monitors.

A gray and blue hull about a mile off their starboard bow caught Alex's eye. "Would you take a look at that? Points to sonar for guessing an old amphib—if that's not an old *Austin*-class LPD, *I'm* a pirate."

"Definitely an LPD, sir." Sue didn't sound amused; her knuckles were white on the controls.

"Might want to stop sounding so Navy, ma'am," Salli said, reaching out to poke Sue gently in the shoulder. "Unless you want them to figure us out in a hurry."

That finally made Sue smile. "Same to you, Senior."

"All right, ladies, we're casual from here on out," Alex interjected. "Dial up five knots and let's see what happens."

What happened was a boarding that took longer than a Navy crew would need—but was a *lot* faster than Alex expected. Within ten minutes *Golden Hind* was alongside their slow-moving civilian submarine, piloted expertly into a position to allow a boarding team to cross over from one boat to the other. The two hulls touched together with only a slight *bump*.

"These guys have definitely done this before," Alex muttered, watching the video.

"You'd barely know that from the rust on that *Kilo*." Sue scowled.

Following her gaze, Alex turned to the monitor showing the view of the the *Kilo*-class submarine that the pirates named *Golden Hind*. The cameras on the Migaloo were pretty sweet; he was going to miss this level of technology when they went back to *Kansas*. But he sure as shit wouldn't miss the sight of armed pirates swarming a civilian submarine.

"That boat's probably as old as you are," he said around the sudden lump in his throat. "Maybe older. Rust is the least of their worries."

"Why don't they use something they've stolen?"

"Warships look more threatening."

"Here they come." Senior Chief Salli swallowed, gesturing at the camera showing three groups of pirates disappearing below decks.

Four of them—all armed with AK-47 and those damned flame throwers—stayed on the beach deck, which Alex thought was a sensible, if regrettable, precaution. He glanced at the chart.

"Set the autopilot for five knots and to stay on this course." Sweat beaded on the back of his neck, and his heart was racing—why the *hell* had he come up with this insane plan?

But his breathing was steady, and that was what mattered. Alex eyed the hatch and counted the seconds, making it to sixty-seven before it cracked open to reveal the muzzle of an AK-47.

"Hands up!" The woman with that thick southern accent shoved her way through the hatch. She had curly brown hair, blue eyes, and the kind of angelic face that made horny men do stupid things.

"We don't want trouble," Alex spoke for everyone. "We're just here to drive."

"Don't worry, we're not after the hired help." She gestured with the rifle. "Do us all a favor and step away from the controls."

"Sure. Just tell us what you want, and we'll do it." Alex didn't have to mime swallowing; his nerves were real, even if he felt like maybe he should be going to pieces and he wasn't.

Nobody could be calm when three pirates—the last stayed outside the hatch, which was annoyingly smart—were pointing guns at them. The other three were all men, but the woman was in charge.

Damn, the cockpit felt tiny with three pirates and three guns jammed inside. Alex tried not to fidget; his neck was stiff.

"Where's the owner?" the chief pirate asked.

"Back aft somewhere." Alex tried to make his shrug look natural. It came off half-convulsive. "Maybe still drunk?"

"Great. You three stay put and do as you're told, and everything will be just fine. Like I said, we're not into ransoming *people*; we just want the boat." She smiled. "People are a nuisance."

"Oh." Sue's voice was a squeak. "That's great to know."

The woman laughed. "Don't you worry your pretty little head."

"You want me to stay and watch them, Danielle?" one of the men asked.

"Yeah. You and Roberto stay put. Patrik and I will go aft and join the others," Danielle replied.

Fuck, Alex thought as Danielle and Patrik exited the cockpit, heading aft. He wanted to warn Paul that two more pirates were coming his way, but trying to use the intercom would probably earn him a quick case of dead.

They didn't expect the pirates to keep them split up, hadn't planned for that. The assumption was always that the pirates would keep their prisoners together. What would happen when Paul and his marines started shooting, but Alex, Sue, and Salli were still stuck in the cockpit?

He kind of wished Gunny had hidden some weapons up here on her wacko scavenger hunt. Alex only shot twice a year to meet Navy qualifications. Sue and Salli did the same. Submariners weren't expected to be good with guns.

Sweat trickled down his back as minutes ticked by. Alex watched the pirates, exchanging a worried glance with Sue. She looked like she wanted to curl up or lash out; neither of them were trained for this.

Interestingly, Senior Chief Salli seemed the calmest, but this was hardly her forte, either.

Damn, Alex wished he'd stuck with a conventional plan and found a way to torpedo these bastards.

Chapter 9

Trapped

L ieutenant Colonel Paul Swanson was used to things not going according to plan. As a Recon Marine, it was pretty much his jam. Hell, even going back to the Wick he adopted the motto of *improvise, adapt, and overcome.* Watching the wheels come off their carefully crafted plan for dealing with the pirates was no big deal.

Now he just had to figure out a way around these guys. Gunny Kochera was a bit of a tech genius as well as being the senior enlisted marine on Paul's team. That meant she'd long since figured out how to hack into *Ranger's* cameras and make their feed show up on her iPad. Paul tracked the pirates in real time, watching them split into four teams while he sat sprawled in a lounge chair in *Ranger's* so-called party bay.

Two fake palm trees towered over him, and the pool bubbled invitingly by his feet. It was a small thing, barely big enough for a dozen marines, but it was still a goddamned pool inside a goddamned submarine. Who did that?

He turned his attention back to the pirates. Lazy rich boy time was over.

Good tactics, he didn't say out loud. He didn't need to. Gunny could pretty much read his mind; she'd been by his side for years and knew this game. He'd say she was like his sister, if the idea of his sister being so tiny *and* his subordinate wasn't so damned funny. No, she was better than a sister. Gunny Kochera was the other half of his brain.

"Here they come," she said in an undertone, holding up four fingers. Then she swapped back to the match three game on her iPad.

Paul grinned before levering himself out of the sinfully comfortable lounge chair. "Okay, boys and girls, party time is over," he said, mindful of the way their visitors got closer with every moment. "Looks like we have sixteen total pirates. Four went forward, presumably to the cockpit. Two other groups of four have split up, and another is staying topside. Stay alert."

His team of nineteen—seventeen, with Sergeant Fernandez back aft in his bunk, watched over by Petty Officer Klusky and Lydia North—did their best to mill around like nervous civilians. The party bay was big, full of televisions, video games, and even expensive artwork, and they'd enjoyed it. But it was hard to fake fun when your mind was on business.

Paul was a little worried about Fernandez, Klusky, and the politician, hidden away in the guest quarters, but the best way to keep them safe was eliminating the pirates quickly.

Two of those pirates waltzed right in the party bay like they owned the place, with their rifles held high. They didn't hold the AK-47s like amateurs, which was annoying, but they also didn't flag each other, and neither had their fingers on the trigger. That last part was encouraging. It meant they weren't going to shoot anyone by accident.

Professional pirates. What an oxymoron. Paul almost snorted out loud.

Gunny was closest to the door, and she jumped up like a startled cat. Eyes wide, she made a show of almost dropping her iPad. She was tougher than Paul, hands down—but she was also good at playing a wilting flower of a woman, one ready to burst into tears when two pirates pointed their surprisingly clean AKs at her.

Not that Gunny would actually cry. Paul wasn't sure she *had* tear ducts.

Her lip trembled. "I'm not—I don't understand. We're not doing anything *wrong*. What do you people *want?*"

Damn, that woman could whine. His turn.

"Hey, bro, we don't mean any harm." Paul put on his best Nervous Frat Boy smile. He'd never been a frat boy—Norwich didn't have fraternities—but he liked to watch brainless college movies. He stepped forward, hands outstretched. "Take what you need, and we won't get in your way."

"That's funny, because we want your boat." One of the pirates laughed.

Both were shorter than Paul by almost a foot, wearing identical sneers. One man was blond and the other brown-haired; beyond that, he didn't take much note of anything other than their suddenly itchy trigger fingers.

So much for professionalism. Facing less-disciplined adversaries was almost comforting; Paul was used to this. More worrisome were the two outside—one dark-skinned woman and an

Asian man—peeking their heads in. They had good overlapping fields of fire from out there.

Yeah, that was a problem.

"That's not cool, man," Paul said, letting his voice shake. "Where are we supposed to go if you take our sub?"

The blond guy laughed and gestured with his AK. "That's what life rafts are for."

Paul's jaw dropped, and it was only sort of an act. "Way out here?" They weren't in a shipping lane, and while Paul didn't know a ton about nautical navigation, he knew that it was a big damned ocean. "How will anyone find us?"

"Not our problem, beefcake."

"Now, c'mon..." Paul took another step forward, just enough to bait them. Little men always liked bullying big ones—and Paul *knew* he was big.

Yep, sure enough, here one came, shoving Paul back with his AK-47. *Not smart.* If the idiot did that again, Paul was going to steal his weapon and break it in half.

No, he couldn't afford to show his hand too soon. The plan was to get all the pirates below decks before jumping them, then trade space for time if things got nasty. Paul tried not to grit his teeth. Confusion and fear were a better look.

He made a show of stumbling when the little blond shoved him. *Target One*, Paul's brain christened him, mostly for his tougher-than-you sneer and the eager glint in his eye.

"C'mon what?" Target One laughed. "What'cha gonna do, big guy?"

"Whoa, easy there." Paul held his hands up in classic surrender. "We just want to make sure we can make it home again, all right?"

"Keep thinking like that and you'll be fine," the brown-haired one said. His smile wasn't friendly. It was tight and sarcastic, but at least it wasn't cruel. This one looked at them like they were *just business*, and that made him Target Two.

"Danielle and Pratik are heading aft to search the cabins, Manuel," one of the pair outside stuck her head in to say.

"Thanks, Kimmy," Target One—apparently, Manuel—replied. Paul filed away the name in case it mattered later. Targets were easier to kill, if it came to that.

His eyes slid left to meet Gunny's. The video they watched earlier made it look like four pirates went forward to the cockpit. Now two of them were searching cabins—not something he could allow—and two others remained up forward with Alex. Shit, this was not going according to plan.

Time to improvise.

He arched an eyebrow. Gunny's lips twitched in response.

"You two eye-fucking over there?" Target One asked, jerking his AK up in what he probably thought was a threatening manner.

Paul just noticed the way it pointed the muzzle at the ceiling *every fucking time*. He almost smiled. *Do that again, sunshine.*

"Oh, ew." Gunny looked ready to vomit. Was she that good of an actor, or was he that gross? Her voice shook. "That's...that's horrible."

"Save it, darling. Pirates of old would have *so* done much worse to you."

She cringed. Paul stepped forward again, now the earnest friend. "Hey, we don't want none of that."

Up came the AK. "You just don't know when to sit down and shut up, do you, macho man?" Target One sneered. "I'm gonna have to—"

The moment the AK-47's muzzle was high enough that it wouldn't shoot him, Paul reached out and ripped it straight out of Target One's hands. He didn't get as much resistance as he expected. Target One yelped in surprise and dove after it, and Paul's knee smashed into his kidneys. That was followed by a left fist to the face, and Target One went down.

Target Two never saw Gunny coming; Paul couldn't track what she did, but Two never came up again from a broken neck.

Unfortunately, the two *outside* the door were quicker. Sergeant Sanders was fast enough to grab the AK off one of them—Target Three let her weapon poke too far through the door—but Target Four almost shot Sanders for the effort. Sergeant Lin slammed the door shut before he could.

Two down, two to go.

Paul ejected the AK's magazine and pocketed it, throwing the rifle itself to the floor. Who wanted Soviet junk when Gunny had an Easter egg hunt of good weapons scattered all over the boat?

"Grab some weapons and let's move, people!"

The unmistakable sound of gunshots carried well in a metal tube; Alex heard the distinct *ping ping* of 7.62×39mm cartridges firing all the way from the cockpit. He knew it wasn't the Marines, too. They were loaded with rubber bullets, which were far less likely to poke holes in a civilian submarine.

"What the fuck?" One of the pirates—Roberto, their leader called him—went sheet white.

"Looks like their employers back aft got stupid," the other one said, reaching for his radio. "Danielle, this is Martin. All okay back there?"

"Fuck if I know. Sounds like Manuel did something dumb. *Again*." Danielle's voice was scratchy on the cheap radio. "Get the crew topside and offload them to a life raft. We'll deal with the morons."

A cold chill ripped up Alex's spine. He tried not to worry about Paul; marines were supposed to be able to take care of themselves, and Paul was badass enough for an entire squad. But if they were dumped off in a life raft—worse yet, *several* life rafts—*Kansas* would have to break off hunting the *Kilo* to rescue them.

Shit, what if the *Kilo*, the Migaloo, and their mothership went in three separate directions? Or even two? Their plan depended upon the *Kilo* and the mothership going the same way. *Kansas* couldn't split herself in half.

"Let's go," Roberto said, gesturing for Alex, Sue, and Salli to follow him.

Sue and Salli both glanced at him, and Alex nodded. They were out of options.

But Alex's feet refused to move, like they were rooted to the floor. Mind racing, Alex sorted through ideas at lightning speed. He couldn't fight; there were no weapons in the cockpit. He couldn't talk his way out of this, not with pirates ready to shoot them. And fifteen years' training as a submariner was summarily useless.

Or was it?

"Hey, buddy, let's go," Roberto said.

Alex's eyes flickered to the navigational plot, measuring distances. They were connected to the *Kilo*, but only by a few lines and a small gangway. The mothership was to starboard, not too far away. He couldn't measure exact distance without using the controls on the display, but he didn't need to, did he?

He hesitated. Squirmed sideways. And just as he was starting to fear nothing would happen, Roberto shoved him.

It wasn't a terribly *hard* shove, but Alex made a show of stumbling right. He caught himself on the ballast control panel, flailing as dramatically as he could with his left hand.

Meanwhile, his right hand punched in the emergency dive command, and the Migaloo dropped like a rock.

The deck disappeared out from under Paul's feet like jumping out of an airplane. But he'd done that a ton of times—enough that he stopped counting after a hundred—so he rolled with the motion and rocketed for the door. His M27 Infantry Automatic Rifle came up, and a powerful kick ripped the door straight off its pretty gold hinges.

Paul surged right; Gunny, one step behind him, went left. *Pop, pop!* Two rubber bullets hit the rightmost pirate—the woman—straight in the face. The next one struck her in the chest and took her down. Paul didn't look to see if she was dead. It was enough that she wasn't moving.

The other pirate hit the ground two seconds later, courtesy of Gunny's expert shooting.

"Take second squad after the aft group," Paul snapped. "I've got the cockpit. If no one finds group three before we get that done, we'll hunt them after."

"Aft, aye," Gunny replied. "Sanders, pop to!"

"Aye, Gunny!"

"Lin, you and your team are with me," Paul said. "Mind the friendlies as we roll forward. The squids might cry if we shoot them."

Sergeant Lin, a lanky woman with dark green eyes and even darker skin, grinned. "No shooting squids, aye, sir."

"Shea, you're on security. Watch these yahoos and make sure they don't creep up behind us!"

"Aye, sir." Sergeant Shea was a stout man who never complained. Not even about being left out of the fun stuff.

Paul moved forward along the Migaloo's starboard side, with seven marines on his heels. He was reasonably confident that the pirate leader—Danielle—was aft of the party bay. Gunny could deal with her, and she'd probably find that third team back there, too. In case she didn't, Paul kept his M27 up and ready.

His long strides ate up the ground quickly, past the ping pong tables, twin marbled jacuzzis, and the giant circular table with aspirations of being owned by the next King Arthur. He tackled the forward ladder, shimmying up it one-handed with his rifle leading the way, eyes peeled for more pirates. No way was he letting his Rook Buddy get shot by some two-bit Blackbeards.

Particularly not when he was pretty sure the boat's current dive was one hundred percent Alex's fault.

But a distraction was a distraction; the pirates *had* to be confused. If he was lucky, they were disoriented, too.

Alex always gave great presents.

"What the hell did you do?" Roberto shook Alex, hard enough to bounce him right off the console, which was an *excellent* excuse to move his hands over the control panel.

He had to do this by eye, guessing the angles—but Alex's fingers tapped wildly, flying across the touch screen, turning the Migaloo to starboard and bumping her speed up. Roberto, not expecting the acceleration, stumbled, then snarled:

"Step away from the controls! Right now!"

"Sorry!" Alex made a show of skittering back—and it wasn't hard to let his eyes go wide with the AK-47 waving in his face—and stuck his hands in the air. "I tried to catch my balance, and—"

The butt of an AK hit him in the gut, hard enough to make Alex double over and see stars. Wheezing, he clutched at his stomach. He wasn't acting, now.

"Hey!" Sue was at his side, catching his arm, by the time Alex's vision cleared. "He didn't mean it, okay?"

Roberto glowered at the controls before looking up at Sue. "Fix it."

"I don't know how to drive. I just work the sensors." Sue's skin was pale and her eyes wide, but her clever words were code for *I don't know what you did, boss, so I'm staying out of the way.*

"Same. It's all him and autopilot," Senior Chief Salli said from just outside the hatch.

Alex straightened slowly. Damn, he wanted to lose his last three meals, and wouldn't puking on a pirate be nice?

Roberto turned his glare on Alex, crossing his arms. "Fix it. Or I'll shoot you and call someone up here to do it."

Yep, this cocky little shit had no idea how to drive a submarine. That was great news and meant the second half of Alex's plan just might work. Or get him shot.

What a pleasant thought.

Alex shivered. "I'll get right on that."

Eighteen knots. Three minute rule says we'd travel eighteen hundred yards in three minutes. Math whirled through his mind; Alex didn't dare look at the clock or the exact range to the mothership. *It hasn't been three minutes, but I don't really need that long, do I?*

Roberto's radio crackled.

"What the hell is going on up there, Roberto?" Danielle's voice asked.

"Idiot freaked out and hit the controls. Fixing it now," Roberto said. He gestured with his AK and put the radio down. "Aren't you?"

"Yeah." Alex nodded. "Just getting my bearings."

This would have to be good enough. First, Alex brought the Migaloo's speed down to ten knots. Anything faster could be suicide. Then he slowly brought the bow twenty degrees further to starboard, looking at the surface sonar picture.

"Ballasting now," Alex said. "Ten degree up bubble. Stand by to surface."

Had Roberto known anything about surfacing a submarine, he might have noticed the Migaloo's autopilot warning blinking red on the screen **CONTACT IN PROJECTED SURFACE RADIUS**. Heart pounding, Alex acknowledged the alarm with the click of a button...and counted to five.

Then his finger slammed down on the **EMERGENCY SURFACE** button and the Migaloo rocketed upwards. Alex, Sue, and Salli stayed on their feet. Roberto and the other pirate did not.

Chapter 10

Outside the Box

M aster Chief Casey happened to be watching on the periscope viewscreen when it all went down. *Kansas* lurked just beneath the waves about a mile aft the *Kilo* and the Migaloo, both to keep an eye on their crew and to spring the trap when the time was right. Casey was a little surprised they hadn't gotten a radio call yet—how long did it take for Marines to shoot up a handful of pirates?

Then shit started happening in a hurry.

First, the Migaloo went under in what was definitely a planned dive. However, it sent the *Kilo* alongside her into a flurry of activity that meant that the *pirates* had no idea it was coming. *Kansas'* watchstanders laughed at that one, because there was no sailor alive who disliked the idea of pirates getting caught unaware and going for a swim.

"Poor fuckers," Casey said without a shred of pity.

"XO's up to something," Lieutenant Lee Kang, *Kansas'* Weapons Officer and the current Officer of the Deck, said with a grin.

"No doubt." Casey looked around. "Anyone want to take bets on what?"

"Gambling's against regs, COB." But Kang laughed as he pushed his glasses up his nose. "I'll ignore your little racket while I call the captain and tell him what's up."

"Be sure to ask him what his bet is, sir."

Casey wasn't really interested in gambling. Sure, he liked the casinos well enough when he had time, but it wasn't really what he'd call a habit. There were easier ways to get free drinks. But bets among friends and shipmates were another thing. They *all* knew that Lieutenant Commander Coleman liked thinking outside the box so much that he frequently went and forgot the box existed.

A couple minutes ticked by. The pirates' *Kilo* putted around on the surface, trying to pull their guys out of the water—Casey counted four of them in the drink—and didn't dive. Just when Casey started to worry that the XO *wasn't* up to something, and the pirates had gone and stolen that million-plus buck civilian boat, movement caught his eye.

Movement. Yeah, that was a word for this goat rope.

It wasn't the Migaloo's bow breaking the surface. He couldn't see that; instead, he saw the pirates' mothership bouncing *out* of the water when the Migaloo came up under it. Casey could imagine the hellacious scream of metal-against-metal as the two tried to mate. The Migaloo ground to a halt, shuddering once, twice, four times like a demented creature running headfirst into a wall—it was stuck.

The mothership yawned to starboard and rocked before settling out at ten-degree list. The aft end of the Migaloo stuck out like a weird ass whale tail, half submerged, half buried underneath the mothership's well deck. Casey's jaw dropped. "What the fuck?"

"Did they just do what I think they did?" Kang asked.

"Fuck me." Casey shook his head. "Those old LPDs have flat bottoms, so they ain't gonna sink, but is he out of his *head?*"

"Can that Migaloo survive hitting something that hard?" Kang leaned in for a closer look at the periscope viewscreen. "Civilian submarines aren't exactly built for ramming speed."

"No shit."

"Looks like the XO's getting creative again," Commander Rothberg said, striding into control. He shrugged. "But it is a damned good way to keep the mothership and the *Kilo* from going in opposite directions."

"Yeah, but those guys look *pissed*, Captain," Casey pointed at the *Kilo* as it picked up speed and headed towards the mothership.

"I believe that's our cue." Rothberg smiled. "Officer of the Deck, set Battle Stations, Torpedo."

"Set Battle Stations, Torpedo, Officer of the Deck, aye!" Kang relayed the order to the Chief of the Watch, and soon the rhythmic *dong-dong* of the general alarm filled *Kansas'* hull.

Dong-dong, dong-dong, dong-dong.

"Set battle stations torpedo. I say again, set battle stations torpedo," the Chief of the Watch ordered over the 1MC, or general announcing system. The alarm donged for several further seconds. "All hands man your battle stations."

Alex was no marine, but he also wasn't an idiot. He was the least phased by the Migaloo's sudden crash, and when Roberto's AK-47 bounced out of his hands and across the deck, Alex dove for it. He reached the weapon before Roberto even groaned in surprise, and spun around as the other pirate tried to get up.

"Drop it!" Alex brought the AK-47 to his shoulder. It felt weird compared to the M-4 the Navy used for training, both lighter and balanced more towards the barrel.

The pirate froze but didn't lower his weapon. Alex's heart pitter-pattered weirdly, tried to jump out of his throat, and his finger drifted to the trigger. He didn't want to shoot someone, but—

Pop-pop!

Two rubber bullets hit Roberto in the chest and he went down with a howl, the pistol in his hand clattering to the ground. *Pop-pop!* The next two hit the other pirate in the back, and he faceplanted into the cockpit deck, gasping and moaning.

Alex stared.

Blinked.

"Easy with that AK there, bro," Paul said from the doorway.

Alex looked at his old friend. The words took a moment to penetrate; he shook his head, trying to clear it. Paul's smile was gentle as he walked over to take the AK-47 out of Alex's hands.

"Why don't you let me take care of the things with the bullets?" Paul smiled.

"Yeah. Good idea." Alex still felt like his heart was somewhere up between his ears, but he tried to swallow back the desire to hide in a corner and shake. "You get the rest of them?"

"My team's back aft doing just that." Paul shrugged as a pair of marines followed him into the cockpit. With two twitching bodies, three sailors, and three marines, it made for a tight squeeze, but Alex was glad for the company.

He was even more glad when the marines hauled out the two pirates, both of whom were semi-conscious and bleeding. He turned to Sue and Senior Chief Salli.

"You guys okay?"

"A little shaken, but we'll be fine, sir," Sue said.

Senior Chief Salli laughed. "Maybe more than a *little* shaken. Please tell me you surfaced under the mothership on purpose, sir. I'd rather think you're batshit crazy than stupid."

"Yeah." Alex coughed out a laugh that hurt his too-tight chest. "That was on purpose. Figured it would stop them from running away."

"It knocked the hell out of us, too." Paul grinned. "But since Marines recover and improvise faster than pirates, it worked out pretty well."

"How long until you get the rest of them?" Alex asked.

"These two make six, with six more to go, assuming the four topside went overboard when we dove." Paul keyed his radio. "Gunny, Swanson. What'cha got?"

"Four down, two cornered. Wait one."

"Aye."

Turning to the controls, Alex tried to put the thought of two pirates running free in the Migaloo out of his mind. The civilian submarine wasn't that big—less than half the size of *Kansas*—and it wouldn't be hard for the pirates to get forward to the cockpit again. But Paul was here, along with what looked like an entire squad of marines outside. Alex should trust them to do their jobs.

Damn, his hands wanted to shake.

"Looks like we have a little flooding up forward," Sue said quietly, studying the hull integrity display. "Auto damage control closed the doors, though, so we're okay."

"I guess those safety features work, huh?" Alex shoved his hands in his pockets. It wasn't like he could drive the Migaloo out from under the mothership's hull yet,; they still needed to trap *those* pirates.

"And this sucker's sturdier than I gave it credit for, too." Salli grimaced. "Going to be a mess topside, though, sir."

"Tell me about it. Here's hoping they don't garnish my paycheck for the damage."

The Gertrude crackled. "Unidentified *Kilo*-class submarine in the vicinity of four degrees, forty-one minutes north, sixty-five degrees, fourteen minutes east, this is U.S. Navy submarine eight-one-zero. You have been caught in the act of piracy. Remain on the surface, heave to, and prepare to be boarded. If you submerge or attempt to flee, you will be fired upon, over."

Sue snickered. "The captain sounds pissed."

"Might be because I wrecked the pricey luxury sub." Alex felt his grin go lopsided. "Or might just be that he hates pirates."

"Who doesn't?" Salli asked.

"You gonna get us out from under their mothership so I can board the *Kilo* and arrest the rest of the fuckers?" Paul asked conversationally. "It's going to be hard to do that from here."

"Picky, picky." Alex shrugged. "Maybe start with the mothership?"

"Sure, if there's a way from here to there."

An hour later, Paul's marines swarmed the mothership and took another ten pirates into custody. This group was quick to surrender, particularly after the marines reloaded with real bullets. Danielle Thayer's capture took the wind out of their sails. She gave up without a fight when Gunny Kochera and Sergeant Sanders threatened to catch her in a cross-fire.

The crew of the *Kilo*, despite knowing that *Kansas* had a torpedo with their name on it, held out for another hour. By then, USS *Hampton Roads* (CG-78) was close enough to put a helicopter overhead. By the time the cruiser came over the horizon, the *Kilo* surrendered.

After some quick negotiation, *Hampton Roads'* boarding team removed the nine remaining pirates from the *Kilo*. Another team from *Hampton Roads* headed over to the mothership to take command from the marines; an excellent idea since Paul Swanson couldn't be trusted to drive anything bigger than a kayak.

Meanwhile, Alex carefully submerged the Migaloo and backed it out from underneath the mothership. Much to his surprise, the Migaloo's hull integrity held long enough to drive her into the mothership's well deck. Getting the boat inside was tricky, but once they got lines over to the *Hampton Roads* sailors inside, Alex nestled the Migaloo against the port side of the well deck, not far aft of the hole he created.

Fortunately, said hole didn't extend into the well deck. It had damaged some of the mothership's ballast tanks, and ruptured one empty fuel tank, but overall, the damage was slight. The Migaloo just hadn't hit fast enough to cause major flooding.

A young-looking Lieutenant wearing a *Hampton Roads* ballcap greeted Alex as he crossed from the Migaloo's deck to the well deck platform. The mothership was indeed a former *Austin*-class amphibious ship; the crest proclaiming her old name of USS *Nashville* was still on the bulkhead.

Alex glanced around. Ex-*Nashville's* well deck was cavernous, and the damaged Migaloo wasn't the only civilian sub in there. Two of the four subs they'd stolen from Weeper's Undertow were there: one Triton 3700 and a Migaloo M4, the little sister of Alex's "own" Migaloo M8.

The lieutenant saluted. "Commander Coleman?"

"Guilty as charged." Alex stole one last glance back at the Migaloo—*Ranger*, Paul kept calling her. That little civilian boat was his first command, and man, he really had mangled her front end.

"Captain Rothberg's on the horn for you." The lieutenant was shorter than Alex, with dark hair and eyes. She extended a bridge-to-bridge radio with a smile.

Alex grinned. "Here's hoping it's not about the damage I caused."

Feeling guilty was hard. They'd captured the Deep Sea Devils, recovered two stolen civilian submarines, the pirates' primary attack submarine, *and* their mothership. Surely a little damage to the Migaloo was a small price to pay?

"He didn't say, sir." Apparently, a smile did not equate to a sense of humor, or maybe this lieutenant just didn't like joking with strange senior officers. Alex accepted the radio. "Thank you."

"You'll need to go topside to get a decent signal, sir."

"Right." Alex didn't mention that submariners were *always* surrounded by heaps of metal. He just headed to ex-*Nashville's* flight deck.

The air topside was clear, and the sky was bright blue. Realizing it was barely noon left Alex dizzy. How had so much action happened in such a short time? Less than three hours ago, he was on a submarine being boarded by pirates. Now the pirates were all either dead or prisoners.

He scanned the horizon, spotting *Kansas* on the surface off the mothership's port quarter. *Hampton Roads* was alongside the *Kilo*, and most of Paul's marines were scattered around on the mothership's deck. The rest would be below guarding the now-imprisoned pirates.

Taking a deep breath, Alex lifted the radio. "Eight-one-zero actual, this is mothership, over."

"Actual here, Alex." Rothberg's voice came back immediately. "How you holding up?"

"It was a bit hairy there for a few, sir, but we're all in one piece." Even if that was hard to believe. "I'm never going to call standard patrol ops boring again, though."

He could hear Rothberg's laugh across the high-frequency circuit. "I bet you aren't. You up for some more interesting stuff before coming back to boring and normal?"

"What, you got another group of pirates for us to trap?"

"No, but someone's got to drive that *Kilo* to Diego Garcia, and I'd rather that be submariners than letting *Hampton Roads* make a mess of towing it in," Rothberg replied.

Now that was interesting. A thrill ran through Alex—sold to civilians or not, a *Kilo* was still a military submarine built by Russia. There were *Kilos* in various navies across the world, including America's enemies. Sure, the design was old, and U.S. intelligence had unearthed almost every secret about them decades ago. But *driving* one, learning about those secrets from the inside, was way better than reading about them!

Hell, Alex thought *diving* into a sunken *Kilo* was the closest he'd ever get. Getting to play with a *Kilo*, even if it was just for the four days it took to get to Diego Garcia, was a dream come true.

"When do we leave, sir?" he asked.

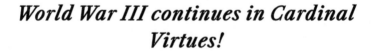

World War III continues in Cardinal Virtues!

As a growing author, every review means the world to me, so if you've enjoyed this story and are willing leave a review, please head over to Amazon if you would. I absolutely appreciate it! Thank you so much for reading, and I hope to see you again!

Also, if you've bought this book without joining my mailing list, please do so - you'll get a free copy of a short story, *Pedal to the Medal*, set in this same universe!

CARDINAL VIRTUES

WAR OF THE SUBMARINE: BOOK 1

R.G. ROBERTS

War of the Submarine

This is the prequel to the *War of the Submarine* series. War of the Submarine continues to follow Alex and the crew of USS Kansas as they find additional trouble—and then into the opening acts of World War III. While the first several books of *War of the Submarine* are available in ebook/paperback/hardcover, you can almost always read ahead in the serial version! Check out the serial if you want to be the first to read this exciting series.

World War I was the war of the battleship. World War II was the war of the aircraft carrier. World War III will be the war of the submarine.
Undersea technology has changed the world, and every nation wants territory. No one wants war—or plans for it—but a series of unrelated incidents, mix-ups, and greedy grabs for ocean-floor real estate escalate straight into a shooting war that no one

knows how to stop...one that engulfs the Indian
Ocean and threatens to spill out towards the rest of
the world.
Old alliances are overturned and new ones form, with
the Grand Alliance of the U.S., U.K., and Australia
facing off against Russia, India, and France. Caught in
a three-way civil war, China is on the outside looking
in, but minor nations are forced to pick sides in the
war no one expected to come—and no one knows
how to win.
For his part, Commander Alex Coleman is pretty sure
that heroes don't explode coffee creamer fireballs
and hijack cruise ships—but let's not talk about that
where the admirals can here; one already hates him
and that's quite enough. He's also certain they don't
end up with a boat old enough to drink and his crew
a few beers short of a six pack. No one expects him
to make a difference...until the enemy gets a vote.
Conventional submariners rarely make history.
Submarines that make history rarely survive.

If you're interested in joining my mailing list, you can
get a free copy of the short story *Pedal to the Medal*,
set in the WOS universe.

About R.G. Roberts

R.G. Roberts is a veteran of the U.S. Navy, currently living in Connecticut and working as a Manufacturing Manager for a major medical device manufacturer. While an officer in the Navy, R.G. Roberts served on three ships, taught at the Surface Warfare Officer's School, and graduated from the U.S. Naval War College with a masters degree in Strategic Studies & National Security, with a concentration in leadership.

She is a multi-genre author, and has published in military thrillers, science fiction, epic fantasy, and alternate history. She rode horses until she joined the Navy (ships aren't very compatible with high-strung jumpers) and fenced (with swords!) in college. Add in the military experience and history degree, and you get A+ anatomy for a fantasy author. However, since she also enjoyed her time in the Navy and loves history, you'll find her in those genres as well.

You can find R.G. Roberts' website at www.rgrobertswriter.com or find all her links at linktr.ee/rgroberts. From there, you can join her newsletters! Joining the newsletter will get you a free novella, set in either the War of the Submarine or World of the Legacy universes (or both, if you like both genres). Newsletters are a twice-a-month affair, so there won't be a ton of spam in your inbox, but you'll be the first to hear about sales, get sneak peeks of new writing, and get to read a few subscriber-only short stories, too!

Also By

War of the Submarine

Before the Storm

Cardinal Virtues

The War No One Wanted
Fire When Ready (September 2023)
I Will Try (Coming Soon)
Read the serial version of *War of the Submarine* on
Kindle Vella and get to start *I Will Try* (book 4) before
anyone else!

War of the Submarine Shorts
Never Take a Recon Marine to a Casino Robbery
(subscriber exclusive)

Pedal to the Medal

Stories of the Legacy

Shade

Night Rider

Legacy Shorts:
Prelude to Conquest (subscriber exclusive)
The First Ride (subscriber exclusive)
City of Light (coming soon)

Alternate History

Against the Wind

Caesar's Command

Other Works

Agent of Change (Portal Sci-Fi with an Alternate History Twist)

Fido (Cozy Fantasy Serial, high on humor)

Printed in Great Britain
by Amazon

33092021R00076